The Mountain's Mate

Salt Planet Giants Book One

Sara Ivy Hill

Contents

About This Book

He'll move mountains for his mate...

When Patrek, a giant Skarr, hires a human for a covert mission, he doesn't expect a female to take the gig. Nor does he expect his long-dormant mating instinct to ignite for someone so tiny! When the heist goes awry and they're forced to hide out together until the heat dies down, the close quarters reveal that, though they're vastly mismatched in size, their hearts are a perfect fit.

To escape with his freedom, Patrek must flee the city. But leaving her behind will break him. Can he convince her to take a mountainous monster as her mate?

The Mountain's Mate **is a steamy, fated-mates alien romance with a huge helping of size-difference!**

A shorter version of this story was published in the *Big Feels* monster romance anthology. If you want to skip to the new material, it begins in Chapter 13.

Content Guide

The Mountain's Mate contains scenes, references, and tropes that may be unsettling to some readers. Please check the content guide before reading to ensure you have the best experience.

If you have more specific questions about the content of this book, please email me at saraivyhill@gmail.com! I'd be happy to elaborate further on any areas of concern.

Happy reading!

SARA

DEPICTED IN SCENES

Hunger, Killing, Violence

REFERENCED

Addiction,   Animal   Abuse/Neglect,   Child Abuse/Neglect, Death of Spouse, Family Separation, Sex Work, Vampirism

TROPES

Alien Planet, Forbidden Relationship, Hurt/Comfort, On the Run, Rescue, Size-Difference, Touch Her & Die

For the space sluts who get it:

Bigger isn't always better,
but this time it definitely is.

Chapter 1

MAJA

The line was too long at the butcher shop. When Maja finally had the small packet of meat in her hand, the last hint of reddish daylight had given way to the aquatic, wavering glow of Salaan's two moons. By the twins, she wished she was already behind the thick, steel door of her apartment.

She avoided the main streets, hurrying down the tight alleyways that zigzagged through the Salt District. The neighborhood wasn't the usual haunt of most Nightborn, but you could never be too careful.

Some of them still practiced the old ways and hunted for their meals.

It was eerie, being out this late, without the protection of the sun. She hadn't been since—she couldn't remember. She quickened her steps until she was almost running, her breath coming in sharp animal pants.

There were other humans still out, of course, but they were marked—if not by a collar with their employers' name, then by the pockmarks and yellow eyes of a tzat addict. There were only a few like her, unbound humans who tried to be invisible as they hurried to reach the safety of their homes.

Hurried as much as they dared, anyway. Too slow meant you were prey. But too fast also drew the wrong kind of attention.

When she reached her squat, plain building, fear crashed and shattered in her chest like a swarm of glasswings. She found herself squeezing the meat so tightly that blood ran through her fingers and pattered onto the sidewalk, betraying her path. It wasn't until the rolling door thundered shut behind her and the lock slid succinctly into place that she let out her breath and gave the poor butcher's packet a break.

She headed down the concrete stairs toward her basement apartment. The comforting noises of the building's maintenance tunnels echoed up to greet her. Most people wouldn't be grateful for such a lullaby, but Maja had spent enough time on the streets to appreciate every ordered hum and grind of the furnace and water pumps. The sounds meant warmth. They meant a roof over her head every night. They meant sleep that was truly restful because it wasn't flavored with fear.

"Give me that!" Xakov's voice startled her, and she dropped the meat at the bottom of the stairs, inadvertently foiling his swipe to grab it from her hands. She swooped it up and skittered away from him until her back was pressed against the wall of the basement hallway.

"It's mine!" she said hotly, clutching the messy packet to her chest and eyeing the door he was blocking with his body. One more door, *her* door, and she'd be truly safe. He tilted his head in the creepy Nightborn way that made the back of her neck prickle.

He sniffed the air. "How does a feedbag with no collar afford djumjum steaks, hmm?"

"I don't know—actually *work* to earn the credits?" Her blow landed. The gray-blue skin that marked him as half-human flushed deeper, and his withered wings flexed.

He stalked toward her until she could feel his hot, coppery breath on her face. She squeezed her eyes shut against it. "Until you're caught up on rent, every credit you spend comes out of *my* pocket. My patience is worn thin, *Maja*." He spat her name like an insult, *Mah-zhah*, his tongue unable to form the sounds properly around his long, sharp canines.

She ducked under his arm and dove for her apartment, slamming the door behind her and releasing the security bar across it with practiced speed. Xakov screeched outside and hammered his fist against the steel. But even his ring of keys wouldn't open it now.

"If you don't pay up by the end of Manna-moon, you're out!" he called through the door. When she didn't answer, he added, "I know you have someone staying with you. I hear you talking through the pipes. If I catch you, I don't have to wait until you skip rent again. I can turn you out now."

"I talk to myself!" she shot back. She was pleased when her voice didn't betray the crushing level of terror she felt at the thought of being on the streets again. She couldn't let it happen.

Then there was only silence outside the door, silence and the hum and grind of the building's guts. In the corner, Carra rustled in her box, and Maja pressed a finger to her lips, cautioning her not to make a sound. Xakov was still out there in the hall, even if he was pretending to be gone.

Finally, the faint *tem-tem-tem* of footsteps sounded from the stairwell, and she let herself relax. "You can come out now," she whispered.

Carra unfolded her two long, scaly legs and stood up, surpassing Maja's height when she stretched her slender neck up into the air. She nuzzled her hooked bill into Maja's hair and preened her like a chick.

Maja took the opportunity to check how the gharial's wing was healing, walking her fingers down the coracoid bone, testing it with gentle pressure. Carra flinched, but only the briefest shudder. The bone felt solid. Now it was just a matter of rebuilding the muscle, the veterinarian had said.

Hence the meat. It was a splurge Maja couldn't afford, but it wasn't like she had enough credits to pay rent before the stop at the butcher shop, anyway.

"Do your stretches while I make dinner," she urged the bird in a low voice, her eyes darting reflexively to the door.

Carra protested with a few lopsided flaps and then obeyed. Gharials were quite intelligent, far more so than the dockworkers who shot them with salt pellets to keep them off the catch would admit. During one of her delivery runs, Maja had found the injured bird crumpled beneath a pier after such an attack and smuggled her to the veterinarian in a spare carra-root sack.

That's where last month's rent credits had gone. And this month's, too.

She probably should have killed Carra and eaten her, Maja reflected as she unwrapped the modest strips of meat and began slicing them into even thinner pieces. That's what her mother would have said. Feed yourself first.

But as she watched the gharial carefully exercise her injured wing, performing the strengthening sequence the vet had outlined with faultless execution, she didn't regret it. Any of it.

Carra deserved to fly again. To feel the tips of her white wings brush the brine as she searched for her sustenance beneath the waves. To find a strong mate, hatch chicks on the hazardous rocky island where the gharial colony nested, out of reach of predators. Safe. Free.

Maja blinked, her vision going fuzzy as stinging tears suddenly invaded her eyes without the excuse of onions. She scrubbed them away with her sleeve and scooped the steak slices into a bowl. She dropped it in front of the Carra. The gharial dipped her beak into the bowl and plucked out a strip of meat. But instead of gulping it down, she dangled it over Maja's head, a coo in her gullet.

Maja laughed silently, pressing her lips together. "I am *not* eating raw djumjum. It's for you."

Carra froze a moment, one fathomless black eye regarding Maja with disapproval, before tilting her head back to swallow it. She tried again with the second piece, like Maja was a recalcitrant hatchling, but gave up by the third, gobbling down her meal with satisfied, throaty chirps.

Maja helped herself to a ration bar, curling up on the bed—the only furniture in the one-room apartment—to nibble it and think.

She still had to figure out how to come up with two months' rent in two days. Her usual daytime delivery jobs weren't going to cut it. Unless she wanted to rent out her womb for the next year, she'd have to work nights, too.

She pulled out her datacom and slid her fingers over the dark screen to wake it. The Graygig app stared back at her. She opened it and weeded out all the postings tagged with feeding or breeding. She would not give any more of herself to sustain the Nightborn.

She was left with few options, none of them legal: transporting "sensitive" goods in dicey neighborhoods, nude dancing at unregistered clubs, some vague ones that were probably peddling tzat. The delivery gigs paid the worst, but she knew the streets and could potentially line up several jobs along the same route.

She added it up in her head. Even if she worked day and night, it might not be enough. She'd have to compromise her standards no matter what.

Tzat-peddling it was, as sick as that made her feel. It was only a few days, though, not forever.

As her finger hovered over the "accept" button, a new gig alert buzzed, lighting up the screen. She checked it. The pay was exorbitant—enough to cover three months' rent, not just two. Hazard bonus, the listing said. No nudity. The only stipulation was body size.

Her size.

She ignored the implications. Or rather, she was resigned to them. She could endure almost anything for one night if it meant that she and Carra kept a roof over their heads, right?

Gig accepted.

Chapter 2

PATREKILGAR

The sweet scent curled under the door before he even opened it. *Female.*

He almost didn't answer her knock. But it was late enough that he feared for her safety, so he opened the door to give her directions. She was lost, obviously. No female in her right mind would be wandering the Warehouse District at this time of night.

"I am a Skarr," Patrek warned through the door panels before he rolled it up. He knew the stories the Nightborn told about his kind, ugly ones woven with half-truths and outright lies. He didn't want her to panic when she saw him and run off the end of a pier or anything. He wasn't good at swimming.

He waited a beat so she could steel herself and heaved the door up with one hand. The tiny human who stared up at him with wide, dark eyes barely reached his hip. The full bouquet of her scent reached him a moment later. She smelled of fear, as he expected, but it was sour and stale. Hours old.

She wasn't afraid of him. Perhaps she should be, in this neighborhood after dark.

"What do you need, female?" he grunted, eager to provide it so her presence wouldn't delay his plans. It was going to be a long night.

Her hand brushed over her brown head fur, and she blinked rapidly. It made her eyes look like the elytra of glasswing beetles, flickering before they took flight. "How did you know that I'm...?"

He took in the rest of her appearance. Her plain jumpsuit was worn and ill-fitting, like it belonged to someone else, someone *male*, and she wore no jewelry or paint to mark her as female. Flecks in a shade or two darker than her skin dotted her nose and cheeks like the first raindrops on dry stone. Was her kind born with those marks, or were they scars that indicated some kind of life experience? He suddenly wished he'd read more about humans in his studies.

"Never mind, it doesn't matter," she insisted, before he could answer that her smell gave her away, not her appearance. "I'm here for the job."

Patrek rubbed his tusks, at a loss for words. *She* was his hired burglar? "No. Too dangerous."

"I accept the hazard pay with gratitude," she said sourly, leaning to look past him into the warehouse he'd called home for the past few months. "Is this some kind of kinky thing? You know it won't fit, so don't even try it."

Now her eyes were on the thick length in his trousers, and the feel of her gaze made him shudder. He couldn't help that his cock's girth was the same as her torso, nor that it never flagged in size. He was simply made that way, although he wished he weren't.

Skarr mating organs were the subject of the worst stories about their species: That their shafts were spiked. That they oozed poison when aroused. That they had fucked their females into extinction. That they hungered to ruin other females in the same way.

None of those stories were true, but he understood that bringing these topics to her attention, even to refute them, would only reinforce their veracity in her mind. He sensed the tension stringing her bones together, the buzz of her pulse rising, and without thinking he cooed to her in the way he might to a skittish Skarr female. It came out rusty from disuse, scraping out of his chest like the dry dregs from yesterday's beer mug.

But it worked.

Her pupils widened as her heartbeat slowed, syrupy, and her sweet smell grew even sweeter. She relaxed in tiny movements, her shoulders dropping slightly, her tiny fingers uncurling from their fists. After a few seconds, when he was satisfied that she'd been sufficiently calmed, he let the noise fade.

"I'll call you a transport. What district do you live in?"

She shook herself like she was coming out of a trance. "I don't need a transport," she snapped, her voice rising.

His gaze flicked down the quiet street. It looked empty, but he knew that ears were listening. "Come inside before someone sends the Authority. You will be safe while you wait."

She froze at the mention of the Authority, and he felt her pulse flap like an injured bird as she gave him a stiff nod and followed him inside. He closed the door gently so as not to alarm her further and then moved to locate his datacom amid the clutter of his workbench.

"Tell me the catch, because so far the main hazard of this gig seems to be wasting my time." She crossed her arms and gave him a scathing look, although he noticed her gaze didn't dip below his belt. She was a brave little thing, but not that brave.

"Hush, female. I'm trying to help you," he muttered absentmindedly, returning his attention to his own mess. He swept aside a stack of schematics to reveal his missing datacom. "What did you say your district was?"

"I didn't say. I don't *need* transport. I need *credits*." Her voice shredded into something ragged, and when he raised his head to look at her, her square, white teeth were bared as she glared up at him. He had spent enough time around feral creatures to recognize her desperation for what it was—a bid for survival. Her desire for credits wasn't greed or even a practical consideration. This was life or death for her.

Her fingertips brushed her chest and then remained there, toying nervously with one of the buttons on her jumpsuit. "I'm Maja. I should have said that."

"Patrek," he grunted. He entered the code in his cashbox. "How much do you need?"

She named a figure so high his teeth clacked together.

He peeled off some credits from his roll and handed them to her. "I don't have it. I'm sorry. I hope this will at least put food in your belly."

"You do have it," she insisted, motioning to the rest of the roll.

His gut tightened. Every instinct in his body was to give it to her. That coo had affected him as much as it had her, awakening something in him that he hadn't known was still there, it'd been hibernating so long—the need to indulge and protect a female, earn her trust and prove his worthiness to be a mate.

He almost laughed. This was no Skarr female ranging her vast territory, in need of gentling. This was a soft little human, an invasive species that, with the protection of the Nightborn, had multiplied so quickly they'd overrun the planet in the three short centuries since their ships crashed on Salaan. Human hyperfertility and general avarice were directly responsible for reducing the Skarr lands to a sanctuary so small that their females could no longer thrive.

This female didn't deserve his care. And she certainly didn't deserve his credits. His stupid mating instincts and hopeful cock would have to remain disappointed.

"These credits have another purpose. One I am not willing to sacrifice." The clock on his datacom caught his eye. He was running out of time. This window of opportunity was going to close, and with it—well, more than credits would be lost.

"Get over yourself," Maja said sharply. "You still need someone to do the job, and I still need the credits. Who are you protecting here? Not me, if that's what you're worried about. If you don't pay me for your purposes, someone else will for theirs. Tell me what I have to do, and I'll do it."

As if the twins themselves were conspiring against him, his datacom chimed with a reminder to pick up the djumjums from the animal hospital. Who *was* he protecting, anyway? His protective impulse toward her, which could only be considered *base*, given that it could not result in a true mating, served no one. If this female wished to risk herself, that was her business.

He didn't like it, but there were a lot of things he didn't like. "Fine. Put this on."

She held up the costume he handed her, holding it between her fingers like it was something dead and rotting. To his surprise, she gasped a pretty laugh. "Djumjum! Figures!"

The happy noise stuck in his heart, quivering there like a prize. Like he'd earned it. He didn't want to know why she was delighted by the costume he'd given her. It didn't mean what it would if she were Skarr, so he pushed the feeling aside. He motioned to the curtained bathing area at the back of the warehouse. "Put it on. When you're done, I'll fit you with the mask."

He changed at the same time, pulling on a tunic over his broad chest and trading out his thin, comfortable trousers for the thicker, stiff ones of the guard uniform issued by his employer, Josefat, who'd hired him a few months ago, mostly as a showpiece.

A Skarr guard was a mark of status that few humans ever achieved, so of course Josefat wanted one.

He had other expensive indulgences, too—like collecting animals for his private zoo. Rare, endangered ones that had no business being kept as pets, let alone bred and sold as playthings. Patrek ground his faceplates just thinking about how he'd been forced to stand by and ignore it. Watch it happening right in front him even when it felt like he'd choke on his frustration and despair.

These were the sacrifices required for a Skarr to achieve his goals, though. Too-snug trousers and patience that would test even a krulloct, and they were known to stalk their prey for years. He buckled his wide belt, and his cock, trapped against his belly, jerked in protest.

"Behave," he hissed at it.

"This is a pet fetish, isn't it?" Maja's uncertain voice came behind him. He whirled his bulk around, startled by the noise, and she scurried back until she was crouched in a dim corner.

"Please, I'll do whatever you ask," she whimpered, her arms crimping to her chest. This time, her fear was fresh, scalding his senses with its wrongness. "Just don't hurt me."

It broke his stony heart. His coo unleashed, unbidden, until she quieted. Careful not to move too quickly, he eased to the floor, halving his height in the hopes that it would intimidate her less, though even seated, he was still taller than her. He reached a hand toward her and beckoned. "Come, little human. You surprised me, that's all."

With a tight expression, she crept out from the corner on all fours, and he was impressed by the illusion. He would've mistaken her for an actual djumjum, at least at first glance. The suit fit, its padding disguising her natural form. The seams were invisible even close up, he noted with pride. On the security cameras, the illusion would be faultless.

"If you allow it, I'll lift you to the table to finish the disguise, and I'll explain the job as I work. We don't have much time to prepare."

A tiny shudder rippled through her, but she settled in his broad open palm, the curve of her hind end fitting perfectly in its cradle. The pads of his fingers braced the small of her back so she wouldn't topple as he lifted her. Her breath sucked in when he stood, her rear djumjum paws paddling in the air until he perched her on the edge of the workbench.

When his hand left her, he couldn't help noticing that her scent remained, faint and sweet on his skin, marking him with her signature.

Chapter 3

MAJA

P atrek's touch was surprisingly delicate as he applied the glue to the back of her front tooth using a swab and pressed a miniscule chip into place with long tweezers. "You'll enter the enclosure with the other animals. I'm confident you will blend in. They are used to humans, so they won't alert to your scent. Inside, you'll locate the impran and place the tracker on her collar. Your suit is equipped with a special claw to remove it from your tooth." He indicated her right front paw.

She flexed her fingers and the claws extended and retracted. She could hardly believe she wasn't looking at the real forelegs of a djumjum. Nor could she believe that she'd get to see an impran in person. Shy, forest-dwelling creatures known for their thin, leathery wings, there were only a handful left on Salaan. "Will she let me touch her in this suit? It's pretty convincing."

"Yes. They're docile. That's why they've fared so poorly. They don't have an instinct for danger." His neck plates creaked as he bent to retrieve a tube from a box on the floor. Maja had seen plenty of Skarr before, but only from the street as they stood guard, their bulk blocking the front entrances of the fancy Nightborn estates they protected. Never any closer than that. As Patrek mixed a different batch of sticky glue, she relished the opportunity to observe him.

Below a bare scalp, craggy brow ridges arced across his forehead and down his cheeks to join with the powerful line of his jaw, framing flinty eyes and a wide nose that had clearly borne the brunt of more than one attack. His broad mouth lacked lips, but he didn't look unkind as he pressed it into a firm line, concentrating on his work. On either side of his chin,

blunt ivory tusks as large as Maja's forearms jutted
out.

It was a warrior's face, though nothing about him
nor his home would indicate he had a tendency toward violence. If anything, the opposite. His table
was littered with scraps of fabric, spools of thread,
an unfinished scarf still on the knitting needles, paper pattern pieces, empty mugs. She couldn't spot
any weapons anywhere, only a bread knife stuck in
a half-eaten loaf that was bigger than her pillow at
home.

Perhaps he, himself, was the weapon and didn't
need anything except his fists and size. But his skin,
the same bronzy-red as Salaan's sandstone cliffs, was
not as rough as she imagined it would be. He looked
like he was carved from a mountain, but he was surprisingly soft to the touch. The plates imbedded in
vulnerable areas were rocky and forbidding, but the
rest of him was pliant, textured hide. He was built for
defense, not offense.

When he'd picked her up, cupping her in his hand,
she'd sensed the heat of his skin through the djumjum
padding, and his gentle grip had made her feel secure.
She hadn't felt so safe and protected since she was

a child in her mother's arms and didn't know any better. Maja wasn't even afraid of being stranded up here on the ledge of his table. She was confident he would get her down as gently as he'd lifted her up.

She held her breath as he painted the edges of her face with the glue in careful, ticklish strokes, then smoothed the mask down with the very tips of his fingers. Djumjums had narrow-set eyes, so it obscured her vision somewhat, but it had good ventilation for breathing, so she didn't feel claustrophobic. She practiced opening and closing her mouth, and the mask stretched with her jaw like it was part of her.

"Comfortable?" he rumbled, a sound that settled in her belly like a heavy meal, hot and satisfying.

Rather than agree, she snorted in her best imitation of a djumjum. He rocked with laughter that flooded her with more warmth. Why his approval of her joke pleased her so much, she didn't know. Faintly, she heard his datacom chime with an alert, and his laughter stopped.

"Do you understand the task?" he asked, suddenly cold and agitated as he attached his datacom and keys to his belt. "Repeat it back to me."

"Act like a djumjum, go inside, find the impran, place the tracker on her collar," she recited dutifully. It sounded simple, but it couldn't be. *Simple* didn't earn hazard bonuses. Her heart rate picked up, and her skin prickled all over inside the costume. "And after that?"

"Hide among the herd until I whistle for you. I will take care of the rest. No need to fear." He made that intoxicating noise again, the one that made her bones feel like jelly.

Suspicion cut through the haze of safety. Was he lulling her into complacence so she didn't ask too many questions? He might be planning to abandon her there after she did his dirty work. That could be the reason for the overgenerous hazard bonus. Maybe he never intended to pay out, and it was just an enticement to take the fall.

But the fall for *what*? Trespassing? It barely qualified as a crime. Something else was going on.

"What do you want with the impran, anyway?" Maja knew they were illegal to own and therefore expensive, but not as expensive as the fee being offered for the gig. He could just buy one. That should have been her first clue that something was off.

He gave the barest shrug. "It's valuable. I'm going to pick you up now, if you don't mind." He waited for her nod before he actually did it, and still it was a rush, being swept down to the floor like that in one motion.

When her legs stopped wobbling, she followed on his heels, practicing her four-legged walk. "Why not just steal it, then? Why a tracker?"

"No more talk," Patrek grunted as he led her out a side door to where a black and green transport marked with a swirling gold "J" was parked in the alley. He opened the back of it and motioned her inside. She clambered up but paused when she saw the open-doored cage that rested in front of her.

Once she entered it and he shut that cage, there was no going back. She'd have to trust him. For some stupid reason, she did. That scared her more than anything.

They don't have an instinct for danger. His words about the impran swirled inside her head. Was that her? Was she the stupid docile animal who would let a predator cage her?

"You don't have to do this, Maja," he said, his voice textured like sand slipping between stones. "You know I'd rather you didn't."

Hearing her name from him did something to her. Strengthened her. Chased away her fear. It was obvious this job was important to him, but he was giving her a choice, even now.

She crawled into the cage. The sound of the door latching caught in her throat, but rather than panic, she closed her eyes and rested, gathering her courage for what was to come. The transport hummed along the city streets. Lamplight flickered against her eyelids, but she kept them firmly shut until she felt the vehicle stop.

She scooted toward the back corner of the cage when the door opened, letting in the voice of a Nightborn veterinary assistant, who gave chatty medication and surgical recovery instructions, and Patrek's answering rumble over the hoots and snorts of the two leashed djumjums that bounded around his ankles. Before she knew it, animals had been loaded into the cage with her, and they were off again.

In the tight space, the djumjums bunched close to her, giving her a good view of the bandages around their freshly cropped ears and the burn-circles where their horn buds had been cauterized. They took turns snuffling every part of her with their wet noses and then, satisfied they'd learned what they could from her scent, lay down, wedged one on either side. Their breathing slowed as they relaxed into a half-sleep, and hers slowed along with it.

The comfortably snug ride was over too soon. The door opened again, bright light hit her, and through her squint she saw Patrek's mountainous silhouette reach for the cage.

"Good luck, little one," he murmured as he let them out inside a gate and then retreated behind it.

She was alone. Well, as alone as a djumjum in a herd of other djumjums can be. A vortex of warm bodies pressed against her and the other two returnees, circling and whistling high-pitched greetings. She snorted back at them, and the tight crowd relaxed, the djumjums drifting off in pairs.

Maja needed a buddy, too, she realized, or she'd stand out. Patrek had warned her about security cameras, and she noted them, high up on poles around the perimeter of the pen. She was being watched. She couldn't stop acting like a djumjum even for a second.

She trotted after another animal while she got her bearings, following it from the dim, grassy paddock area to a well-lit row of empty metal troughs. It pressed on a pedal in front of one, releasing a cascade of smelly treated grain, and began gobbling up the food.

Her stomach turned, but she pretended to eat, dipping her snout into the trough and raising her head to "chew" while she scanned for the door. What had seemed like simple instructions when Patrek had spoken them—*go inside*—felt overwhelming now that she was on her own.

A large stone building formed the fourth side of the djumjum enclosure, but smaller wooden structures dotted the paddock as well, casting long shadows across the grass. Which one was *inside*?

Her friend burped and ambled away, so Maja followed her, poking her head into the little huts they passed as she tried to maintain the unnatural, four-legged gait. The buildings were dim inside and lined with straw that had been stamped into tight, round nests. Sleeping areas, many already occupied with snoring animals.

The stone building was her goal, then. As they neared the unbroken façade, she spotted a djumjum-sized door at the base. It was on some kind of sensor, sliding up when an animal stepped on the ramp and then back down behind it. Periodically it opened to let a djumjum out, along with a beam of yellow light from the interior. The mechanism must work the same on the inside.

Abruptly, "her" djumjum veered into a sleeping hut, grunting as she turned in circles before curling up on the floor, snout between her front paws. Maja took a deep, straw-scented breath and let it out again. She peeked out of the hut, marking her path to the entrance, and then, as casually as possible even though her chest was tight with anticipation, strolled toward it.

When she touched the ramp, the door jetted up with mechanical precision, and she hurried through it so it didn't guillotine her on its way back down. Inside, the warm yellow light flooded a comfortably human-sized hallway with a patterned tile floor. Maja had to resist the urge to stand up and walk on two legs to peer into the glass enclosures that lined it in case there were cameras here, too.

It was an exotic animal collection—a zoo, maybe. A well-kept one from the look and smell. Creatures of all kinds inhabited the enclosures. Long, lithe serpents. Fuzzy, long-tailed tree hoppers. Even a glass-wing colony. Most she'd never seen in person before, just heard about, because they were nocturnal. The impran had to be here somewhere.

Though she longed to pause and really soak up the fascinating experience of seeing some of the rarer animals up close, observe their behaviors and quirks, she had to play djumjum. She scanned each enclosure as carefully as she could through the mask, swinging her head around for a full view through the narrow-set eyes. She reached the end of the hall without spotting any sign of the impran's leathery wings, and a frosted glass door opened for her automatically.

Now she understood why the djumjum door led here. It looked like a small veterinary clinic. Though it didn't appear equipped for anything complex like a surgery, the walls were lined with glass-fronted cabinetry, and the surfaces were all antiseptic metal that reflected dully in the low lighting. Thankfully, it was unstaffed due to the hour.

She jolted when a robotic treat-dispenser beeped and spit out a yellow nugget when she passed. Clever. The djumjums, trained to visit the clinic on their own to collect treats, probably didn't balk when the nuggets were accompanied by examinations or inoculations.

Honestly, the treat smelled good. Her stomach rumbled, and she rationalized that, if the cameras were watching, she ought to eat the nugget. So she did. It crumbled in her mouth, sweet and buttery, as she explored the rest of the clinic. It was so much better than the ration bars she usually ate that she was only faintly embarrassed to be eating livestock treats.

In a small back room, Maja spotted the impran. The remains of the treat turned to ash between her teeth when she got a good look at her. Unlike the thriving collection of exotic species that lined the hall, the poor thing was wedged in a cage so small she couldn't spread her wings.

Not that she'd be able to even in a larger cage. She was strapped into some kind of tight, rubber harness designed to prevent it—and had been for a while. Her skin was patchy and inflamed where the restraints had rubbed off her short body fur, and her huge, black eyes had a gray film over their surface as they stared, unfocused, at the single small window, even though it was too dark for Maja to see anything outside.

The impran had obviously been mistreated and was terribly ill. Even someone without veterinary training couldn't miss it. It was the lack of hope in her pointed little face that did Maja in, though. When she saw it, her doubts about the gig vanished. Whatever the Skarr giant had planned for the impran, whatever cage he was going to keep her in, it *had* to be better than this.

Time to place the tracker. She wrangled open the cage door and flicked out her special claw to remove the chip from its hiding place on her tooth. But she paused when she noticed the small water dish inside the cage was empty. Completely dry.

Cursing the clumsiness of the costume's paws, she ripped them off, dropping the djumjum pretense so she could stand and fill the water dish in the small sink nearby. The impran didn't even turn her head when she replaced it.

By the twins, the creature wasn't going to last another day.

"You have to drink, sweet thing," Maja whispered, dropping back to all fours, the tiles chilly under her naked palms. "You won't make it until Patrek finds you, otherwise."

The impran gave a slow blink with her huge, limpid eyes before inclining her head in a nod and resting it back against the bars. If Maja didn't know better, she'd think the impran was politely indicating her gratitude and declining—the water or her own survival, Maja couldn't tell. She was definitely reading too much into it, the same way she liked to think that Carra was mothering her when she preened her hair even though it was probably only an instinct triggered by its texture and color.

Just in case, she whispered, "Do you—understand me?"

The impran nodded again.

"Do you—speak?" This time, the impran wagged her head back and forth, clearly saying *no*.

Realization raked over Maja, clawing through her skin. The impran wasn't just intelligent. She was sentient. A sentient being was restrained and caged without water or food!

Maja started to explain about Patrek and the tracker and offer a flood of reassurances that help was on its way, but then she stopped. She couldn't guarantee what would happen to the impran. Though she had an unreasonable amount of faith in Patrek, it was based on nothing but an instinct, too, as fallible as Carra's mothering impulse. She had no real idea of his plans nor the timeline for those plans. And the impran didn't have time. This couldn't wait.

She took off the creature's too-tight collar and unbuckled the harness that restrained her limbs. Shakily, the impran stepped out of the cage, stretching her wings out to their fullest extent with a whimper that indicated their soreness.

"Drink," Maja insisted. "Then we're getting you out of here."

The impran nodded, dipping her nose in the clean water while Maja went out into the other room and coaxed another yellow nugget from the treat dispenser. She returned and offered it to the poor thing. The impran gulped it down and croaked something in a chirpy language Maja couldn't understand. Thanks, perhaps.

"It's nothing. I'm sorry this happened to you," she said. Then she went to the window and unlatched it, easily lifting the starved impran to perch on the sill. The creature gave Maja one more nod and launched silently into the dark.

Maja had never felt happier in her life. Not even the alarm that began to blare could quench her burning joy that the impran was free.

Chapter 4

PATREKILGAR

When the alarm sounded, it was almost a relief. Since his shift began, Patrek had been arguing through his com with Vilbo, the Nightborn assigned to watch the security cams that night. This was partly to distract him from any view of Maja as she entered the collection house, but it was mostly because the saltlicker wanted to harvest an animal tonight instead of tomorrow, the day Josefat had scheduled.

Djumjum were expensive creatures to keep because they needed space and a lot of feed to thrive. But as expense was no object for Josefat, he preferred to maintain his own little herd to supply his table, lavishing the animals with every luxury.

That didn't spare them the inevitable execution, though. There was a weekly harvest day. The Nightborn guard only wanted to do it early so he could take the offal home to feed his bloodwed human rather than leaving it for the guard assigned to the next shift.

"I have kids with her!" Vilbo said through the com, like Salaan needed more human-hybrid brats crawling on it. Patrek tried to tamp down his bitterness. What was done was done. No more Skarr would be born. The only thing he could do now was make sure no other species suffered the same fate.

Normally, Patrek wouldn't get involved in something like the harvest schedule. He wasn't eager to draw attention to himself, given that he had his own ulterior motives for his employment. But he couldn't risk Vilbo randomly choosing Maja as this week's harvest animal, so he'd been threatening to tell Josefat of the unsanctioned change to the schedule when the alarm pierced his skull.

Patrek's momentary gladness at the distraction was immediately overwhelmed by panic. Had she been caught? "What's going on?" he asked urgently through the com.

He could hear Vilbo muttering to himself as he looked through the security system for what had triggered the alert. "Window open in the collection house," he finally said. "Probably nothing, but I'm initiating a lockdown until we can sort out what happened."

The alarm switched to a different blare, one that called more guards to do a sweep of the estate, and Patrek tensed. Maja would be discovered. And Josefat was unlikely to call in the Authority to deal with her, given that he was trafficking in protected species. No, he'd question her himself or call in a Council crony. Patrek had seen his methods—there was no way the soft little female could withstand them.

"I'll go check the animals," he said. He shut off his com so Vilbo couldn't protest and ran for the djumjum enclosure. He had to get Maja out.

All the security lamps were on, bathing the paddock in their harsh glare. Careful not to lean on the fence with his bulk, he scanned the area and whistled.

A few sleepy animals poked their noses out of the huts to see what was going on, but none stepped toward him. By the twins, he'd made the human's disguise too convincing; he couldn't tell if any of them were her from this distance.

He was running out of time. If she was still inside the collection house, the lockdown sequence would soon trap her there. He strode over the fence, barely pretending to inspect its perimeter as he barreled toward the large stone building. He could hear the mechanism engage just as a djumjum snout appeared in its opening.

Her.

He had barely enough time to lunge as the door slammed down, but he wedged his fingers underneath it to stop it sliding home.

"Quickly," he barked, straddling the ramp and stepping closer to the building to block the view of the cameras, as her scent, sweet and unmistakable even through the full-body suit, reached him.

"I'm stuck," she panted, her voice slightly muffled by her mask. Her heartbeat leaped, frenzied, in his ears. He could feel her writhing between his knuckles as she struggled to squeeze through the narrow opening.

He heaved upward, hoping to buy her an inch or two more, but the mechanism had locked. Too strong, even for a Skarr. Unless he wanted to break down the stones of the wall itself, there was no more space to be had.

"Try, little one."

"I *am* trying. It's not my fault djumjums have fat asses." She grunted and hissed and grabbed his wrists, trying to pull herself free. She abruptly released him, along with a jumble of words. "Go. Before they catch you. I won't say anything, I swear. Just do me a favor, if you can. Find my apartment. Salt District, building G12. Basement. Let Carra out so she has a chance."

He heard pain lance through her voice. He didn't know who Carra was to her—a mate? No, a mate wouldn't be locked away. A child maybe. He ground his teeth and tried again, straining with all his strength against the door. No use.

"Slide out of the suit," he ordered, no longer invested in maintaining the subterfuge. If she was caught, the secret was out, anyway. He heard the hidden fastening of the costume unclasp as she obeyed him, the glue tear away as she peeled it away from her head and down her body. He glimpsed a stripe of her bare back in the gap between his forearms and shuttered his imagination against the image of her shoulders and chest exposed to the night air.

"Still stuck," she panted. "Too tight. *Go*." She pushed against him—against his *cock*, making his blood surge and heat—urging him to leave her. But he couldn't. Or wouldn't.

If he let the door go, she wouldn't just be caught, he realized. She'd be crushed. As the raised voices of approaching humans reached his ears, he grasped for the only solution at hand. Literally.

"Unbuckle my belt."

"What?!"

"I would do it myself, but my hands are occupied," he said wryly. "Trust me. It's the only way. Do as I say, and I'll get you out."

He felt her fumble with the buckle and then pull it free, her hands hesitating on his waistband.

"Take it out and stroke it," he directed, turning his face up to the night and squeezing his eyes shut. He didn't dare look down and see her touching him. This wasn't about *that*.

"You want that *now*?" Her voice was thick with shock.

"No. Yes—it produces oils." His face plates ground together as he grimaced with embarrassment. "They'll ease your way out of the suit. By the twins, female, *hurry*."

She was silent, and then her hands dipped into his trousers, pulling him free, and he felt the glide of her tiny palms over his many olje, the oil-producing glands villainized as the spikes that ruined the Skarr females. Ironic that their purpose was the opposite—to soothe and comfort.

It felt so good he nearly swallowed his tongue. "That's enough," he choked out.

She knew what to do with it. He felt her twist and shift as she applied his oils to her body where it was trapped in the djumjum disguise. He braced harder against the door and was gratified when he felt the sudden change in pressure that meant she'd slithered free.

"The suit," he gasped, muscles straining. When he saw it flick past in his peripheral vision, he let the door go. It crashed shut with a terrible noise, and the shouts of the guard team grew louder. He had to hide her now. They wouldn't make it to the huts.

He pulled the waist of his trousers as wide as he could. Then he plucked her up from the ramp, doing everything in his power not to register the sight of her nakedness, and tucked her into them. "Hold on," he directed her, glancing over his shoulder to make sure no one had seen them.

She balked. He knew she would, so he supplied the answer already on the tip of his tongue. "No one will notice a little extra bulk in a Skarr's trousers, now, will they?"

He felt her arms wrap around his upright shaft just beneath the head, and one leg hooked over the base. With her ankles locked together, she gripped him with her thighs, her weight pulling him to one side. It was an excruciatingly pleasant sensation. He couldn't adjust her or dwell on it, though. There was no time.

Swiftly, he pulled the pants up over her head and belted around her body to hold her in place against his belly. He pulled his uniform tunic down to conceal her just as the gusts of wind from Nightborn wings hit his back.

"Problem?" Vilbo's voice rang behind him.

Patrek stooped, painfully aware of his cock as Maja's arms squeezed around it, to pick up the flaccid djumjum suit in his arms. He bunched it to approximate a live animal before he turned around.

"Stupid creature got caught in the door," he said, stroking the suit and keeping his voice lazy and casual as he looked down at the guard and prayed to Night Mother that Vilbo didn't notice that his cock was *breathing*. "I pried it out, but it's injured. Guess you'll get your harvest tonight after all."

Vilbo lit up, moving closer to get a look at his prize, but Patrek shrugged him off, cradling the fake djumjum above his head. "Do a headcount," he directed. "I'll take this one to the harvest house. Too heavy for your puny arms."

As he'd hoped, that drew an amused snort from Vilbo, who flew off to count the remaining herd. Its population would be off by one, the one Patrek was supposedly carrying off to be harvested, but it'd take Vilbo long enough to figure it out that there was a hope of getting Maja off the property. Thank Corek that the guard didn't seem too worried about what had set off the alarm.

What *had* set off the alarm?

Patrek headed for the gate, unsure if he could straddle the fence with Maja hanging on for dear life. The feeling of her clutched around him was unbearable. Every step, he jostled her bottom with his thigh, sending her in a brief slide up and down his shaft. Sometimes her chin would bump against the glans, sending a jolt of desire through him that tightened his balls to the point of pain.

She could probably feel his arousal. She must be horrified. But horrified was better than falling into Josefat's hands, he reminded himself. Judging by her pulse that fluttered against his most sensitive skin, her stress level wasn't elevated—no more than it already had been, anyway—so he hoped her dismay at hiding inside a Skarr's trousers would not escalate to trauma.

He took the shortest route to the edge of the estate to spare her further humiliation. Wedging his shoulders between two large shrubs to ensure privacy, he pulled up his tunic and unbuckled his belt to let her out. "Go on, now. I can't guarantee you more than ten minutes of safety, but that should get you far enough that they won't find you."

To his utter shock, she tightened her arms around his cock and shook her head, jutting out her chin as she stared up at him. "No!"

Amusement twisted his mouth as a laugh rumbled out. "What do you mean, *no*? You're going to live in there now?" He reached down with two fingers, intending to gently pry her away from his body. "If you're worried about payment, don't be. I set it to transfer automatically."

She batted his hand away. "I'm naked, you big saltlick! I can't run through the city like this. I won't make it two blocks before I'm sucked dry by Nightborn. Anyway, my keys are at your house. How am I supposed to get into my apartment?"

"Ah." He rubbed his brow ridges. For all the time he'd planned this, pored over his notes to account for every variable, distilled and simplified the plan until it was idiot-proof, he hadn't considered this scenario—a tiny naked female wrapped around his cock, her glare as sharp as a krulloct's claw as she refused to climb out of his pants. "Of course. I'll take you to collect your things."

It was too late for any hope of hiding his involvement anyway. He'd walk to the warehouse, put her in a transport, destroy any evidence of the operation, and retreat to the mountains. At least the impran's tracker was in place, so someone else could carry out the rest of the mission.

He paused, mid-buckling of his belt. "You were successful? You found the impran?"

"Yes?" The hesitation in her voice dug at him.

"But you didn't place the tracker," he finished for her, stones in his guts. She *buried her face* in his cock, sending those rocks in his belly tumbling and dragging a groan from him. "Night Mother, I wish you wouldn't do that."

"Sorry. I'm so sorry—I tried, but I couldn't."

He'd failed. Months of work, wasted. He didn't blame Maja; he blamed himself for not following his instincts and turning her away when she knocked at his door. It would have delayed him, delayed the plan, but maybe on another night, it would have worked.

He swallowed the stone that rose in his throat, finished securing her in place, and with a glance over his shoulder to make sure none of Josefat's guards had noticed him lurking in the landscaping, set off in the direction of the Warehouse District.

Chapter 5

MAJA

She owed Patrek an explanation, not the apology she'd given. She wasn't sorry for what she'd done, even though she could tell he was disappointed, just as she was disappointed to lose out on the payment. Gutted was more like it.

But he was walking now, moving swiftly through the streets, and she didn't dare make a noise under the tent of his tunic, not at night when the Authority had jurisdiction of the city. So she just clung to him and shut her eyes, relaxing into the rhythm of his strides.

It must be so awkward for him, carrying her like this. Her breasts were pressed tight against him due to the tether of the belt around her back. She *had* to put her hands on him, squeeze her legs around his cock, just to keep from flailing and sliding around. Every step rubbed her core against the small, flexible nubs that covered his shaft, which made them gush the oil that she'd used to free herself from the djumjum door. She was bathed in it already, and they had miles to go.

Even more awkward, it felt good. Too good. So good she wanted to rub against him more, not less. Heat built between her legs with every swaying step. It wouldn't take long for her to tip over the edge if things continued like this, and it wasn't right, taking pleasure from him without his consent. He was trying to help her, not fuck her. He wouldn't want her quaking on his cock like a suffocating sea star.

She dug her feet into the crevice between his belly plates and thighs, using the leverage to put whatever space she could between their bodies to spare them both the friction. Her movement made him freeze, and she felt his hand on her back through his clothing.

"Maja," he rumbled. She felt the rise and fall of his breath as he clasped her tight, stilling her movements. Her traitorous body pulsed and throbbed, begging for more, and she felt him twitch, jostling her whole body.

He knew. He had to know. And he wanted her to stop. Though they were both still and silent, the moment was shocking in its raw intimacy, and a burning blush crept from her hairline down to her toes.

How mortifying. What would he think of her after this? She'd ruined his plans and then shamelessly taken pleasure in a dire circumstance that shouldn't have been enjoyable at all. He was doing her a favor and she was just perving on it. Even under the canopy of fabric, she could hardly endure the embarrassment, let alone when she had to get out and look him in the eye.

It didn't matter, really. She would never see him again. But she still felt sick about it, and the shame was almost enough to quench her arousal completely.

He stroked down her back once, the pressure of his hand reassuringly firm, and then started walking again, his movements jerkier now as though he were trying to avoid jostling her so much. The effect was the opposite. Every unpredictable jar zinged through her, ricocheted between nerve endings and set her afire in places she'd never been aware of. The backs of her knees tingled, and her lips hummed with desire.

But at least she had come to her senses and didn't get carried away by it, just clenched her teeth and tried to push the feelings down.

She heard the noise of the rolling door purr upward and then crash down, saw a glow through the weave of the fabric that surrounded her. And then he pulled up his shirt, letting in a rush of cool air and light so bright that she had to blink while her eyes adjusted. He unbuckled his belt and set her gently on the floor without even looking at her.

Not that she wanted him to. Then she might see the disgust in his eyes. She felt like she'd smoked a whole pipe of tzat. Loopy, feverish, and buzzing, topped a good dose of shame.

"There are rags and soap in the back for the mess," he said, already moving to the workbench and gathering things up, shoving them into a canvas rucksack bigger than she was.

She remembered her nakedness then and hurried behind the curtain to where she'd left her clothes and datacom. She climbed on a ladder to use the sink and caught a glimpse of herself in the mirror. Her skin was still covered in a thin layer of Patrek's oils that gave her belly and breasts an iridescent rainbow sheen.

The mess, he'd called it.

It didn't look like a mess to her. It was...pretty. She smoothed her hands over her body, spreading the oil to parts of her thighs and arms that hadn't been in contact with him. It sank in immediately, leaving her skin glowing and impossibly soft. She knew she ought to wash up as he'd suggested, but for some reason, she didn't want to.

Rationalizing that she could get back to Carra faster if she skipped the clean-up, she dressed quickly, using a little water to restyle her short hair. When she emerged from the curtain, she found Patrek with his back to her, feeding papers from his work bench into the warehouse's garbage incinerator. He threw the djumjum costume in, too, which she hadn't realized he still carried.

He was destroying the evidence. He didn't turn around when she cleared her throat, so she spoke to his monolithic back like it was a walled city and she was begging entrance.

"I authorized return of the payment. I'm sorry again that I screwed it up." Maja swallowed hard as she tucked her datacom into the back pocket of her baggy denim coveralls. She'd find some other way to pay the rent. She had to.

His breath huffed out as he threw more papers onto the fire. "That's not necessary. You did your best. My plan was flawed."

She should take the money and go. Even waiting for a transport was stupid when someone was handing her a miraculous credit balance. But the truth was brittle and thick inside her and wouldn't let her leave without revealing itself.

"Your plan was fine. I just didn't follow it," Maja said in a small voice, cringing when he slowly turned to look her in the eye. She spread her hands, begging for understanding. "I'm sorry. I couldn't leave her the way I found her, tracker or no tracker. They had her tied up in a tiny cage with no water. Did you know that imprans are sentient? She *understood* me. I *had* to let her go!" Her last syllables were almost a wail.

"You released her?"

Maja nodded. "Out the window."

He grunted, looking like he wanted to say something. But the look on his face told her the answer. He knew about the impran. And he didn't disapprove of what Maja had done. Not entirely.

"Is that why you did all this? To help free her somehow?" Maja guessed, taking a few more steps toward the giant until the heat from the open incinerator beside him buffeted her face.

He nodded reluctantly, then seemed to decide to confide in her after all. "I work with a group of Skarr that rescue exploited creatures. Not just sentient ones that have been kidnapped," he added. "All of them. The Skarr may be doomed, but we'll protect those we can. We hoped the impran's tracker would lead us to wherever they're being bought and sold."

She groaned. Of course, he had a plan. One more complex than she'd imagined and that served a higher purpose, too. And she'd sabotaged it. "I'm so stupid. I should have trusted you."

"I gave you no reason to." He rose to his full height, dwarfing her again, and closed the incinerator door. Then he reached to brush the top of her head with the flat of his thumb. He jerked it back like it'd burned him. "We didn't realize her health was so compromised. You did the right thing by releasing her. You were clever and brave, and you probably saved her life."

But condemned many others. The thought echoed in her skull until she insisted, against her own survival instincts, "I can't take your credits. Not if you can use them to try again."

"You must." He stared down at her for a long minute before he spoke again. "I endangered you. If I had trusted you with the truth, the plan might have worked. It wasn't your failing."

"Half. I'll take half," she said, unable to look away from his kind eyes. Had anyone ever looked at her with such deep compassion in her entire life? If so, she couldn't remember. "But only because I need it. If it weren't for Carra..."

Recognition flooded Patrek's expression at the name. "Your child?"

"No, she's—" Maja began, but she was interrupted by a shuddering crash against the warehouse door. It came again, rocking her where she stood.

"Hide," Patrek said tersely.

"Who is it?" she whispered. He didn't answer, eyes fixed on the door, so she did as he'd told her, diving behind a stack of wooden crates at the end of the workbench just as the metal buckled and failed.

She balled tight, heart hammering as she tried to shrink into nothing. They'd been discovered. They'd probably both go to prison even though she was the one who'd let the impran go. If she had just followed his plan and placed the tracker, none of this would have happened.

"Where's the creature, Patrek?" a hard, lisping Nightborn voice rang through the space. She bit her lip to hold back the whimper that tried to claw its way out and squeezed her eyes shut. Was it the Authority?

"Gone," Patrek answered calmly. Something scraped against the concrete floor.

The whine of a blaster charging electrified her eardrums. "Don't move, Skarr."

"Settle your wings, Vilbo. I'll come willingly." Maja didn't know how Patrek could stay so placid with a blaster in his face, but his steady voice felt like his hand on her back—firm and reassuring. She had nothing to fear, but still she couldn't crack her eyes open.

A hiss and bright flash through her eyelids, then the smell of burnt flesh. It wasn't until Patrek's pained growl reached her ears that she realized the Nightborn had *shot* him. Her breath came fast and noisy, rushing in her ears.

"Just a little reminder," the Nightborn, who Patrek had called Vilbo, hissed. "Josefat wants to talk to you, but you only need a mouth and lungs to speak. The rest of you is disposable."

Patrek grunted. "Good luck carrying me to the estate, weakling."

The hiss and flash came again, and a muffled groan let her know that Patrek had taken another blaster hit. She couldn't let him do this, sacrifice himself for her mistake. But what good was she against an unarmed Nightborn, let alone one with a blaster?

"Get in the transport." Heavy footsteps let her know Patrek was following instructions. That was a good sign—he could still move. Maybe if she distracted the Nightborn for long enough, Patrek would be able to disarm him.

She uncurled and crawled a few paces under the table so she could see around the edge of the crates. Vilbo—whose dark blue skin said he was pure

Nightborn or near it—had his back to her and his weapon trained on Patrek. Patrek's eyes widened momentarily when he spotted her over the Nightborn's shoulder.

"No," he said, looking right at her, meaning the word for her.

Vilbo squeezed off another blaster round, blinding Maja momentarily. When her pupils adjusted, she saw Patrek clutching his shoulder as blood coursed down his arm, raining onto the floor where it dripped off his fingertips. It reminded her of the butcher's packet, how she'd squeezed it as she ran through the streets, fearful she'd be swooped up by a hunter.

The Nightborn noisily sucked his fangs. "What a waste of good food."

"Come closer and have a taste," Patrek taunted. She begged him with her eyes to stop his game, stop inviting this cruelty. Even a Skarr like him, a magnificent mountain of a being, was no match for the ruthlessness of the Nightborn. They would cut him and cut him until he was whittled to nothing.

She stood up without thinking. "Stop it. Stop hurting him!"

Time seemed to slow for the next few moments. Vilbo's wings snapped out in surprise, and his blaster swung in a wide, slow arc as he turned to aim it at her instead of Patrek. Now behind him, Patrek's flinty eyes went black. In two steps he had his good hand around the Nightborn's skull. A millisecond later, Vilbo's neck was broken, and he lay in a crumpled blue heap on the floor.

Maja sputtered and nearly fell to the floor herself. "Why—why did you do that?"

"He was going to shoot you. Are you hurt?" Patrek had reached her and cupped her back with his good hand, the one that had just ended someone's life. He turned her around, inspecting her.

"You could have broken his *arm*. You didn't have to kill him."

"I did," he said darkly as he let her go, seeming satisfied that she was unharmed. "He saw you. Even if we escaped, sooner or later, Josefat would come looking for you. This way, they're still only looking for me."

Maja swallowed hard. She didn't know who Josefat was, but from Patrek's tone, she didn't want to know. She should have stayed hidden, like he told her.

Then that Nightborn would still be alive, and Patrek would still be a simple thief, not a murderer.

She couldn't dwell on it. If she thought any longer about how this was her fault, too—*all* of this was her fault, every single thing that had gone wrong tonight—she'd collapse and be even more of a burden to him. "We should go before the Authority shows up."

Patrek grunted in agreement, already cleaning and bandaging his blasted shoulder. When he finished, he picked up his datacom and, to her shock, threw it into the incinerator. She made a disbelieving squeak.

"They'll track it," he explained, swinging his enormous rucksack onto his good arm. Right, they were criminals now. "Salt District, building G12?"

"You remembered." Maja hardly remembered herself. She felt as fragile as a gharial egg, like she'd crumble if one more weight was placed on her.

His thumb skimmed the top of her head, and he made that lovely noise, the one that softened her and strengthened her all at once. "Let me take you home, little one."

Chapter 6

PATREKILGAR

He hated that he couldn't carry her. It would attract too much attention if he did. But he had to fight every possessive Skarr impulse to scoop her up and cradle her against his chest as they began their trek across two districts on foot.

By the twins, she wasn't his female! He only had one arm worth anything, anyway. He couldn't very well carry her and protect her with it at the same time, so he followed behind her, close enough to act in her defense but far enough back that no one would suspect they were together. He would guide her and guard her and then leave her in safety before he made his way back to the mountains.

They kept to the alleys, too narrow for most Nightborn wings and barely wide enough for Patrek's shoulders. He kept scraping his injured side on the buildings. Every time the grating sound of plate-on-stone rasped out, Maja shuddered, her pulse leaping like a longtail through the trees.

He couldn't imagine her horror and disgust at this point. She'd been subjected to so much, most of it his doing. Whatever hazard pay he'd attached to the job couldn't begin to cover the hazard of being plastered up against a monstrous cock while its owner tried not to come in your face.

He'd been too ashamed to look at her when she'd emerged, blinking in the light and shining with oil, from his trousers. And if that weren't bad enough, minutes later, he killed someone with his bare hands right in front of her. Showed her what a monster he really was.

With any luck, her mind would disperse the ugly details of the night into something murky and undefined, a dim repository that would protect her from what happened tonight. From memories of *him*. He wasn't helping her forget by sticking around.

But he could not rest easy unless he saw her home himself. He would always wonder if she'd made it back safely, and he'd have no way to contact her to check—not until he was back at the sanctuary, which would be many days' journey through the forests.

One of his shoulder plates wedged in the crack of a window ledge, sending a sharp spike of pain down his arm, and a screech echoed down the alleyway. He watched the noise reverberate through her, stopping her in the street until she gave a shake of her head and soldiered on.

If he were a better Skarr, he would put her in a transport and head to the mountains now instead of tagging after her like a lost pup. If his goal was to protect her, sparing her his presence would do the most good.

"Maja," he said, just loud enough for her to hear. She paused again and turned, her shiny beetle-brown eyes trapped in the spinnerweb of the streetlamp's glow. He opened his mouth to suggest she call a transport to take her the rest of the way, but before he could get the words out, he caught her scent.

Not her scent. *His* scent. Potent and undeniably his. He'd missed it back at the warehouse because the place was full of his smell. But now, in the salty, clean air of the night, it was obvious.

She hadn't removed his oils.

He didn't know why, and he didn't care. His mating instincts, which he now realized had only been smoldering, ignited to full flame in his chest. He *burned* for her, the air in his lungs so searingly hot that he gasped. It didn't matter that she wasn't Skarr and probably didn't understand the ramifications of wearing his oils. She had accepted his claim, and she was *his*.

"Patrek?" she asked, her tiny brows ridging. "Are you in pain?"

Yes.

"No. It's nothing." He rubbed his shoulder, as though that was the thing troubling him. He could hardly feel it, in truth, because of the fresh wound that had just been torn inside his chest.

Her gaze tugged ahead, never resting as they scanned for danger. "We shouldn't dawdle."

"You're safe," he blurted out. She was, for now. Everyone gave Skarr a wide berth. But he could tell it was the wrong thing to say when her face wrenched into a smile that had none of her precious humor behind it.

"Never heard of it." She turned and walked away, speeding her steps like she was trying to shake him off. Of course, how could she feel safe in the presence of a murderer? It was impossible. So he didn't try to reassure her or explain, just gave her a little more space and kept his eyes sharp. She *was* safe with him. He would make sure of it.

As they entered the Salt District, the buildings grew shabbier and shabbier, the alleys more cluttered with refuse, the Nightborn patrols overhead less frequent. The smell of fear coated everything, layers of old and new terror that tormented his senses with their sour pungency. But even as his discomfort grew, he sensed her relaxing bit by bit.

As they reached G-block, she even gave a small skip before ducking her head and darting a nervous look over her shoulder as if she might be reprimanded for it. This was her home, among the other humans. But he didn't like that she lived here, where so many were miserable. It wasn't right. She should be free and fearless, not cowed and caged.

The irrepressible need to help her swelled inside him. This was what Maja must have felt when she realized the impran was sentient, he realized. He had the same impulse to release her. He should take her with him, out of the city and into the mountains. She wouldn't have to look over her shoulder there, because he could watch over and protect her.

It wouldn't be the same as having her as his mate, but it would have to be enough. At least then her safety wouldn't bite at him constantly.

"You can go now," she said, and he realized they'd stopped in front of an ugly, cracked apartment building marked "12" at his eye level. She stared at her feet, so his only view was the top of her head. "Thank you for—everything."

Everything. Patrek snorted. He was pretty sure she wasn't thankful for any of it except the credits, and those she had earned.

"I mean it. You don't know—" her voice cracked, and she swallowed the rest of her sentence, repeating herself instead. "You don't know."

He started to make his offer to carry her into the mountains, and Carra, too, whoever she was. But before he could get the words out, the citywide sirens started to blare. All the datacoms on the street chimed at once, and Maja pulled hers out of her coverall pocket.

She raised her face from the screen in horror. "They're looking for you. It has your face and your name and everything."

By the twins, he should have called her a transport back when he'd had the impulse. Now he didn't have time to convince her to go with him. She already had the door open and was heading inside, eager to get as far away from him as possible. He couldn't blame her, after what he'd put her through, even though it made his soul ache.

As much as he wanted to, he couldn't linger in front of the building and moon over her. It would lead the Nightborn right to her door. He had to run or prepare to fight an entire Authority squad single-handed.

Running sounded better. He mentally plotted the quickest route to the edge of the city boundary. It wasn't close by, but there, he could disappear into the forest. The Authority couldn't move easily in the trees unless they went on foot, which would slow them down.

"Manna save us, get inside!" Maja's head appeared in the doorframe, and he realized she was talking to *him*. She yanked on the hem of his tunic. "Please, Patrek."

That word, *please*, was like an invisible leash that tugged on his heart. How could he do anything but obey her? He dropped to his hands and knees and crawled into the apartment building's tight foyer.

She locked the door behind him and then climbed over his calf to reach the stairwell. He could tell she was still jittery, little bubbles of anxiety popping off her and needling the inside of his nose. Her voice a whisper, she asked, "Will you fit, do you think?"

He eyed the narrow space. "I guess if I get stuck, we know how to ease my passage."

She laughed and then clapped her hand over her mouth, eyes flicking upward as her cheeks pinkened. Then she turned and hurried down the concrete stairs. He followed more slowly, careful not to clang against the metal railings or scrape his plates against the walls.

His heart galloped in his ribs, but it wasn't from fear of being caught. The sound of her laugh had made a whole flock of feelings take flight. All he wanted to do was coo. Foolish mating instincts.

He made it—just made it—down the stairs, where Maja was waiting by an open door, impatiently waving him inside. This door was much smaller than the building's entrance. He had to contort his body, resting on his good shoulder and pushing off from the stairs with his feet, to slide through the frame sideways, and even then, the top of the doorway scraped his blaster injury.

"Pull up your knees," Maja said briskly, and when he did, she shut the door and blocked it with a security bar. Then she let out a heavy sigh and slid to the floor herself, holding her face in her hands. Her shoulders started to shake, and the refreshing scent of the sea met his nostrils.

Her tears? If she was so distressed to have him here, why did she urge him inside? It didn't matter; he had only one responsibility. He let out the coo that had been lodged in his throat for what seemed like forever. It was deeper and more resonant this time, now that it'd had some exercise.

Maja raised her head and wiped her eyes, a smile curving her mouth, and he realized she'd been laughing, not crying. "I'm glad we didn't have to oil you up to get you through the door. Night Mother, what a mess that would be."

He chuckled at her joke, even as his cock twitched at the thought of her hands on it again. He rolled over to crush the damn greedy beast beneath him, and his knee bumped into a nearby box, sending it skidding. A terrifying cloud of white feathers erupted from the cardboard, heading straight for his eyes. He had just enough time to duck his face under his forearm before it hit him, scraping and clawing and biting like a hailstorm in the darkest night of winter.

"*Carra, stop!*" came Maja's shriek. So this was Carra. Not a child or an elderly friend, but a saltlicking gharial! Why in Salaan did she invite one of the vicious sea birds into her home? Their claws could pierce Skarr plates if they were determined enough.

He did his best to defend against it without hurting the creature, and thankfully, it listened to her, retreating to twine its neck around her shoulders and preen her head fur. He grinned when it trilled over her. She hadn't adopted it. It clearly had adopted *her*.

He sat up, nearly brushing his head on the low ceiling of the one-room apartment, and took in the details of her home. If he stretched out his arms, he could easily touch opposite walls, and his body occupied most of the free floor space. The only furniture was a narrow bed under the high, frosted window. It reeked of solitude.

He sucked in a deep breath to be sure. It smelled only of Maja and the gharial, and he was secretly, selfishly glad that her existence was so lonely. She hadn't invited others inside, only him. And now there was no room for anyone else.

A stupid, possessive thought, pure mating instinct and nothing to do with reality. She was human, he was Skarr. She could never be *his*. Like she'd said when she first saw him—it won't *fit*, so don't even try it.

"Are you all right?" she said, lightly stroking the arch of the gharial's wing. "She didn't mean it. She was just protecting me."

"They're loyal to their mates." He chuckled, swallowing his need for her. "How did you come to own one?"

"She was hurt, but she's healing now. I'll take her back to the docks where I found her when she's able to fly again." Maja offered him a small smile, and it was like a beam of sunlight had pierced the dimly lit room. Pierced straight through his sternum, too. He rubbed it, wincing, and her face fell. "Oh, your injuries. I can't believe I forgot!"

"Don't worry yourself," he began, about to explain that he'd tended them well enough to heal back at the warehouse, but she'd already shrugged off the gharial's preening and hurried to the tiny kitchen in one corner. She rummaged in the cupboards until she found what she was looking for, a small blue box.

She held it up triumphantly and was about to say something when Patrek caught the scent of a Nightborn leaking in from the hall. He held up his good hand to warn her, and her eyes went straight to the door, like she could read his mind. Thank Corek, the gharial seemed to know when to quiet its trills, too. It settled back in the box he'd disturbed, the rustle of its wings against the cardboard like dry leaves.

For a few moments the silence hung heavy over them, until a shuffling scrape was audible outside the door. Maja rolled her eyes even though Patrek heard her heart startle and race at the sound. He longed to soothe her, but he knew the sound was too much risk.

"I know you're out there, Xakov!" she called. "What do you want?"

"I heard noises," Xakov lisped back. "What's going on in there, feedbag?"

"Talking to myself," she shot back. "It's not illegal."

The voice went from velvet to acid. "There's a vicious murderer on the loose, you know. A Skarr. Maybe you should let me in so I can look around."

Maja snorted. "Nice try. I think I'd notice if a Skarr was hiding in here. They're not...small."

Patrek grinned at her as her eyes slid over him, lingering where they hadn't been brave enough to dwell before. Apparently, now that she was acquainted with his cock, it wasn't so scary. Why did that please him so much? Probably because it meant she hadn't been traumatized by their escape. It certainly wasn't because he hoped she'd touch him like that again. He wouldn't ask that of her.

"They're easy to smell, too," Xakov snarled. "I'm not stupid. There's Skarr all over the stairs."

"It's not a Skarr, it's me. I had to take a job at one of the big estates to pay the rent on time. Do you want to know the details? I'd be happy to relate

every moment of my evening and the things I had
to do to avoid being turned out on the streets by my
landlord." Maja's voice held the flat, plain truth, her
exhaustion palpable in the timbre of it.

He shut his eyes against the pain on her face.
Thank Corek, Xakov didn't take her up on the offer.
Patrek didn't think he could bear to hear what she
might recount. It wouldn't be the truth of tonight
but some other, worse truth, something from her
past.

"I expect to see payment in my account soon,
then."

"Before the end of Manna-moon," Maja agreed.
She held her breath until the Nightborn's footsteps
were audible on the stairs, marking his retreat, then
let it out in one big gust, turning her attention from
the door back to Patrek. She eyed his lap. "May I?"

He nearly choked. Of course, she didn't mean
that. Her sights were on his shoulder now. He nodded, unable to trust his voice. She handed him the
box, no bigger than his thumbnail, and climbed up
on his thigh. She stood on tiptoe so she could reach
his hasty bandage, her weight hardly noticeable, and

hummed as she removed it, tutting and whispering to herself.

Patrek held as still as a mountain and breathed in her smell mixed with his, memorizing the combination of his oils and her sweet bloom. He could feel her calming as she prodded and cleaned and applied ointment to his blaster burns.

Something settled inside him, nesting like the gharial in her box. He would let her tend him. She obviously enjoyed it. He could not give her pleasure in other ways, so he would give her this.

Chapter 7

MAJA

Curled on her bed in the dark, the cool moons-light wavering on the ceiling, Maja couldn't help being conscious of the huge sleeping giant on the floor next to her. He wasn't resting near her on purpose. It was just that no matter where he laid in the compact apartment, some part of him would be close by. She could reach out and touch him if she wanted to.

She wanted to, badly. She felt strangely *settled* when they were skin-to-skin, like nothing could hurt her. She'd drawn out the bandaging of his shoulder as long as she could, just to have the contact. The blaster burns had already started to heal and didn't need her attention, not really. But it felt good to tend him, the same way it'd felt good to tend Carra's broken wing.

Like she had a purpose. Like she wasn't just another feedbag.

Her fingers crept to the edge of the bed, itching to extend the inch or two it would take for their tips to brush the rocky plates below the bandage on his shoulder.

"Can I ask you something?" His voice was a husky whisper in the dark. She jerked her marauding hand back and shoved it under her thigh.

"I thought you were asleep," she murmured, glad that it was too dim to show the flush that heated her cheeks. "What is it?"

Patrek cleared his throat. "Why didn't you remove my oils? You could have washed them off at the warehouse. And you could have bathed once we came back here. But you didn't."

The question hung there in the room like a lantern, making her feel terribly exposed in its light. "You can tell?" she asked faintly.

"Skarr have very sensitive noses," he said, a note of
amusement coloring his tone.

Night Mother, what else could he smell?!

"Sorry, I didn't know. I can clean up now," she
chirped, hoping his sensory acumen didn't extend
to detecting her utter humiliation. She swung her
legs off the bed and started for the wash closet, but
he scooted his good elbow to block her path so she
couldn't reach the door without climbing over his
arm.

"Don't. Please, don't." He propped up to look
her in the eye, so close to her that his twin tusks
nearly pinned her to the wall, one on each side of her
waist. The moons-light turned his red-brown skin
a charcoal gray that glimmered slightly, like it contained flecks of precious metals, and his eyes gleamed
as bright as Manna and Corek in his face. "I like it.
I mean—you can wash if you want to. If you prefer
it. But don't do it on my account. I asked because
it's meaningful to Skarr females to leave it on, and I
wondered if it was meaningful to you, too?"

He whispered the last words of his question, and
his hot breath made the skirt of her sleep shift balloon

and lift like it wanted to fly away. She smoothed her hands down her body, avoiding his gaze.

"I don't know why I left it on," she admitted. "I just didn't want to wash it off. I liked how it looked. I liked...the feel. Does that qualify as meaningful?"

"It does to me." He opened his mouth to say more and then shut it again and drew in a long breath through his nose instead. What was he going to say? She was vibrating with curiosity.

"What does it mean to your people? You can tell me," she added, squirming against the wall as his exhale curled around her legs and warmed her core. "I won't be upset by it. I find it fascinating to learn about other species and their habits."

Patrek's mouth quirked. "How can I refuse you, then? When a Skarr female doesn't remove a male's oils after mating, it means that she trusts him and cares for him. That she accepts his claim. Their mingled scents let everyone in the clan know that they're a bonded pair. I never thought—well, I never dreamed I would have the privilege to smell my scent on a female. It was only a wish, one that was impossible to come true now that our females are gone. So I thank you for the gift. I am honored by it, even if nothing can come of it."

Warmth spread over her, a curious sticky ache. "Because you don't want a human mate, you mean?"

"I know it doesn't mean the same thing to your kind," he rumbled softly, his lids falling shut as he took another long, shuddering breath. "But I will treasure the memory of this night for the rest of my life. My oils and your sweet essence in one breath? There's nothing more perfect on Salaan. If you were Skarr, I would—"

He broke off and sat up abruptly, nearly bumping his head on the moons-lit ceiling, and rubbed the center of his chest. He took his comforting warmth with him, and Maja felt the chill reality of her basement home. The safety and security she felt with him were just temporary. Patrek might love her smell mixed with his, but he didn't want a human. He didn't want *her*—only the dream of a real mate. He would leave for the mountains as soon as the Authority lost interest in pursuing him, Carra would fly away when she was fully healed, and Maja would be alone in her cold little life.

Why did that make tears threaten to flow? It'd always been this way, whether she had a roof over her head or not. It just never hurt before because she didn't know it could feel different. He had done this. Shown her a glimpse of some other life that she couldn't live.

Anger welled underneath her sadness as she pinned her arms across her breasts. "You would *what*? What would you do for a Skarr mate that you could never for me?"

His reply was slow to come, and her heart raced as she braced for it. The answer was obvious—his huge cock stood between them, as large as her head and torso and barely contained by his loose trousers. A female of his kind could take it. The thought sent a pulse of heat between her legs as she remembered how his oils had slickened her, sensitizing her breasts and belly as she clung to him. How the little nubs strummed her clit as she slid up and down his shaft. How dizzy with desire she'd been when she tumbled out of his pants after their escape from the estate.

"Maja." Patrek's voice was strained, drawing her eyes up to his face. His expression was etched with pain and the plates in his forehead ground together.

"I smell your need. But I can't bring you pleasure, little one."

"You can," she blurted out, almost whimpering. "You already did, and I'm sorry. I know I shouldn't have enjoyed it. But I couldn't help it. And I wish—I wish I was Skarr so I could give you the same feeling." The admission left her breathless and weak-kneed, like she might dissolve into the floor.

He flinched, his head falling back to expose the armor of his neck, and he ground the heel of his hand against his cock. It was such an unselfconscious, sensual gesture that a bolt of lust seared through her at the sight. When he raised his head again, his glittering gaze pinned her to the wall. "Night Mother knows, it was everything I could do not to spill all over you. It hurts how much I wish I could." He stroked himself once and then, as though he'd thought better of it, he simply gripped it through the fabric and squeezed. Hard.

Maybe it was the moons-light. Maybe it was his oils on her skin. Or maybe it was just the swollen folds of flesh between her legs that were humming and begging for fulfillment after being denied for hours, now that she knew she hadn't disgusted him.

Whatever it was, Maja suddenly felt bold. Her hand crept beneath the hem of her sleep shift and found her clit, circling it and rubbing along one side as she sagged back against the chilly concrete wall.

Patrek's nostrils flared, and he was on his belly in an instant. This time his tusks really did capture her against the wall, his mouth and nose only inches away as he swallowed her scent. "You really wish to know what I'd do to you? How I'd take you and please you and make you mine?"

She nodded, her fingers moving faster, coaxing more and more heat from her sopping pussy. Already, the tendrils of pleasure were spiraling out of her control, pulling her to pieces. "Tell me, quick," she gasped, and Patrek growled against her.

"I would hunt you by your scent. You couldn't hide from me, little one, not even in the deepest forest. And when I found you—"

"You'd catch me," she panted, thrilling at the thought.

His tusks scraped the wall as he pressed forward as far as he could, his mouth almost brushing the fabric of her garment, his breath as hot as hands on her skin. "No. I'd tempt you. I'd bring gifts—ripe fruit to eat and soft skins for your bed. I'd watch over you as you ate and slept. I'd defend your nest from all who'd disturb your rest or do you harm."

By the twins, even better. She melted at the thought of him standing guard all night, his strength at her service. She could be satisfied with that alone. But she had to know the rest, even if she could never experience it. "What then?" Her nipples peaked into tight points in anticipation of his answer.

He growled, still gulping breaths of her between his words. "Then, if you offered yourself to me, I'd pin you with my tusks."

"Like this," she panted. Her clit pulsed, threatened to tip her over the edge, so she pulled back slightly, resuming the wider circles that teased rather than satisfied. She was as desperate to draw out and memorize these moments as he seemed to be. When had she ever felt so safe and desired? When would she ever have this again?

"Like this," he rumbled his agreement. "I'd coo to quiet and soothe you, and then I'd cover you with my oils. Every inch of your body would carry my scent and mark you as mine."

Maja's skin blazed in recognition that she, right now, was already anointed, already marked. Already his, even if he didn't want a human that way. For this moment, this night, they could both pretend.

"You'd beg for me," he continued hoarsely. "And then I'd fill you and rut you and spill inside you. And after, I'd use my tongue to clean you up. Taste your sweetness mingled with mine. Maja, your scent is blooming so beautifully—I can't resist it."

"Then don't. Please, don't." She hardly knew what she was asking for. He couldn't rut her or do any of those other things, but Night Mother, she wanted him to. Her mind was so hazy with the crackling energy between them, she almost believed he could.

She was barely conscious that he was touching himself, too, one arm working frantically beneath him, before his tongue snaked out. She caught a flash of it, purple-gray in the moons-light, before it swiped up the inside of her leg and found her folds, knocking her hand aside to press a broad tip in its place. Her eyes rolled back in her head at the hot, delicious pressure.

Then he *licked* her.

All other thoughts vaporized as his enormous tongue swept over her sex. Again and again, the tiny textured bumps zipped over her nerve endings like an echo of the ones on his cock, probing and tasting and *laving* her with such strength that it lifted her up onto the balls of her feet with each pass.

She didn't last long before she slipped down the wall, his tusks under her arms the only thing that kept her from puddling on the floor. He hummed with delight when she grabbed onto them to stay upright, and the buzz traveled through the squirming muscle between her thighs. She came then, shattering and quaking and biting her own wrist to avoid crying out as she rode his slick tongue to the end.

Chapter 8

PATREKILGAR

Maja's sweetness had him in knots. The flood over his tastebuds when she came made him see stars, it was so good. He wanted her to crawl all over him, cover him in her scent just as she was covered in his, watch him spurt and unravel at her touch. But she was heavy on his tusks, drowsy from her release, so he moved her gently to her bed.

"Rest now, little one. I'll watch over you until morning."

To his surprise, she sat up, bracing herself on wobbly elbows. "What about you?"

His cock bucked in his trousers at the question. He gave the overeager thing a censuring squeeze. "I wouldn't ask that of you. That was enough for me. More than enough."

She sat all the way up, her rumpled head fur silhouetted by the light from the high window. "I'm offering. I know I can't give you exactly what you want, but—"

He tipped his head back and groaned, cutting her off. "You *have*, female. What more could I want than your taste on my tongue and your scent on my tusks so I can breathe it in all night?"

She laughed, the moons-light catching on her flat little incisors. "Oh, I can think of a few things."

"Tell me, then," he ordered gruffly, laying back on the floor and fixing his eyes on the ceiling so he didn't have to see her expression as he reached into his trousers again. "Tell me what I wish for."

She sat a minute on the edge of the bed in silence, and he could hear her pulse quicken when he began stroking up and down his shaft, the head of his cock heating and swelling before he even got two pulls in.

She sucked in her breath when he let it emerge from the confining waistband of his trousers.

He paused, afraid he'd made a mistake. He should have insisted that she sleep. This was too much. *He* was too much.

He didn't even know human mating rituals. Maybe what he'd described about the Skarr ways was bizarre and abhorrent to her. He didn't smell fear, though. He sneaked a look at her face and saw only eager curiosity there.

"You wish to see me bare," she said swiftly, biting her shiny lower lip as though she couldn't keep the thought to herself. She stood up and tugged her white sleeping garment off in one motion, letting it fall to the floor. Her skin was tarnished silver in this light, her breasts casting dark wings of shadow down her ribs. Her belly rounded below, and she had sturdy, graceful limbs despite their tiny size. All soft, all sweet.

"Yesss." He *had* wished for this. His chest heated with longing as he took in her perfect little form. He wanted to catch her in his hand, touch her everywhere, bring her to his mouth and suck her sweetness again. But he kept his clumsy paws to himself and resumed his lazy strokes, enjoying the view that he'd avoided back at the warehouse, now that he had her permission. "So beautiful, Maja. Like a dream."

"This is a dream," she agreed, moving closer and leaning over his side until he could feel the swell of her breasts pressed against the plates of his abdomen. She reached to tug his waistband lower. "You want me to see you, too."

How could he deny such a statement? With a groan, he lifted his hips to slide his trousers free, and he heard her breath catch when his full length was exposed. Her heart sped until it was just a purr in his ears. Too much?

No. Her eyes were wide and wondering but not afraid. Blood swelled her lips, and her tiny, taut nipples pricked with interest as she followed his hand's movement up and down his shaft. She wanted this, too. The pressure built under his palm, begging for release, but he hated that the moment would ever end. He could not have dreamed to have this—her attention, her desire, her scent twining around his tusks.

"You want me to mount and ride you," she said in almost a whisper. Night Mother, Maja might make him come with her words alone. Now that she'd said it aloud, he could think of nothing else but the vision of her legs wrapped around his girth, squeezing him. "May I?"

He tried to give his consent but all that came out was a guttural, needy sound. Trembling, he placed his free hand for her to use as a stepping stool, ignoring the twinge in his shoulder at the movement, and she clambered up to straddle his cock. It bucked underneath her when she swung her leg over it, and his olje gushed fresh oils at the hot press of her folds as she let her full weight settle onto him, her knees digging into his belly. He tried to harness the thing, pressing the tip down with his fingers, but she pushed his hand off with her heel.

"It's mine to tame now." Her voice was low and determined, almost possessive, so he settled back, cupping his hand behind her in case she tumbled from her unbearably erotic perch.

"I'm at your mercy, little one," he assured her. "Do what you will."

She let her hands wander over him, testing and pressing his olje, milking them until her thighs were slick and shiny with their secretions. She touched

them with such reverence and fascination that it was
almost a form of worship.

His mating instinct screamed that she was the one
who should be worshipped, not him, but he was selfish and couldn't bring himself to stop her. Not when
she was sitting atop him like a blossom on a branch,
smelling so sweet.

Especially not when she raised her hands to show
him her shiny palms and then rubbed a fresh coat of
his oils all over her breasts and arms. His hips bucked
involuntarily, and he couldn't help touching her
then—he supported her back so she wasn't jostled
to the floor by the movement, and she leaned into
it, letting him carry her full weight as she drenched
herself in his scent.

This had to be a dream. How else could it be possible?

"My perfect little mate," he rumbled. "My Maja."

And then she started to move, bracing her hands
under the lip of his cockhead and using the leverage
to slide her slick little core over his length. The friction of her folds over his olje made his plates vibrate
with desire. He thought he might rattle to pieces.

It seemed to have the same effect on her—within just a few iterations, she was whimpering and squirming, impossibly delicious and wild. She collapsed forward on him, clinging with her arms and legs just as she had when she was hiding in his pants, and rested her cheek against his glans like a pillow.

"Too sensitive still," she panted, turning her face to plant a wet kiss against his frenulum. "Give me a minute. Your tongue ruined me."

The memory of her taste made his balls tighten, nudging up behind her, and she wriggled her lush little bottom against them. It took all his will to keep from thrusting against her. He didn't have to, anyway. She did it herself, digging her toes into the crevice of his thigh and launching herself forward. Floating on a viscous layer of his oils, her whole body slid until her breasts caught against his cockhead, stopping her momentum. The wave of pleasure that dashed over his senses made him gasp for breath.

He was only vaguely aware of Maja whining as she tried to writhe back down to her starting position. "Help me," she demanded.

His hand settled over her back, covering her like a heavy blanket. He squeezed her gently, feeling her relax under his touch as her spine molded to his palm. Then her little feet prodded him, demanding his obedience, so he followed her lead, sliding her up and down as she directed him with her impatient kicks.

At first he hesitated to use her like this, fucking her whole body as he trapped it between his hand and his infernally hard cock. But as her sweet scent unfurled even more, and her satiny, oil-softened skin slid over him, he relaxed into a shameless rhythm, punctuated by her pants and little animal sounds.

She wanted him. He could sense it with every breath he took. She didn't pity him or fear him or wish he was something different. She was the one who sought to mount him and ride him and tame him. He shuddered, remembering her whispered suggestions.

"Patrek!" Maja gasped when he moved beneath her. Under the weight of his hand, he felt her convulse against him, her hips rocking to rub against his olje, and she gifted him a second orgasm, murmuring his name.

He reveled in the pulses of her small body, brushing his thumb over the back of her neck and her delicate shoulder blades until she was no longer wracked with pleasure. When the tension eased from her limbs, she rubbed her face against the head of his cock like she was marking him with her scent.

Manna save him.

His instincts hadn't been misplaced when they ignited in the street—this was *her*, his mate. He didn't ask her to offer him sanctuary when the Authority hunted him, but she had, at great risk to herself. She'd accepted his claim, signaled it by wearing his oils even after she knew what it meant. She'd taken her pleasure from him—now twice. He couldn't give her everything a mate should, but by the twins, he'd try. His cock swelled and begged with all he wanted to give her.

"I'm going to spend," he warned, but it just made her clasp him tighter, her arms and legs snugly circling his shaft, the squeeze making his tusks ache with the effort of holding back. "I don't want to drown you."

"Yes, you do. You want to drown me in it," she said sleepily. "Come for me, Patrek. Please."

That sweet plea did him in. With a roar as silent as he could make it, he came in scalding jets, covering his abdominal plates and splashing over his hand and Maja, too. Wave after wave of pure, filthy, impossible joy washed over him. A mate. *His* mate.

Chapter 9

MAJA

S he was covered in his warm, sticky seed, virtually swimming in a pool of it as Patrek's strong fingers stroked and massaged her back. Without thinking, she slipped her tongue out to taste it. It tasted how it smelled, creamy and sweet, like milk with a hint of honey and something else, a warm spice like elannot bark.

He sucked in a breath and when she raised her head to look at him, she saw he was watching her, his brow ridges furrowed. Was he surprised by her?

Or did he have regrets? She wouldn't let him, not so soon. Not under the moons-light.

Something willful and wanton overtook her, and she dipped her tongue in his spend again. A breathy moan escaped her as she rolled it over her tongue, memorizing his flavor.

"I knew you'd taste good," she murmured against the soft warmth of his cock. "Better than any Manna-moon cake. I could live on it."

"Is this part of the human ritual?" he asked. "Tasting in the way that the Skarr scent?"

"No," she answered honestly. "I just want to remember this for later. For when you're...gone."

He made that sound, that delicious purring growl, and scooped her up onto his chest, where she could feel his heart thundering through his plates. Then he pulled the sheet from her bed and used it to gently clean her and then himself.

She melted into him. He was so warm. She didn't want to move to her narrow bed unless he was uncomfortable like this. She sprawled there on his chest, tracing the irregular shapes of his plates with her fingers, feeling their rocky edges and occasionally dipping between them to the thin, delicate skin underneath.

"Tomorrow—" he began after a lengthy silence, but she interrupted him.

"Not yet. Don't talk about it yet." She wasn't ready to stop pretending. She wasn't ready to let him go, and in the morning, the truth would be laid bare in the light. He couldn't stay. He was wanted for murder by the Authority, for one. And he was Skarr—huge and noble and so far above her, both figuratively and literally, that she'd be beneath his notice in the street. Here, in the dark, she could have him for a little longer.

Patrek rumbled his assent, his thick fingers still toying with every part of her, so mammoth and so gentle. "Tell me of your clan, then," he said.

"My clan?"

"Your people here in the city. I know nothing of your life. Your ways."

"You know everything of my life," she whispered into his plates. "This is my life. I earn credits in the daytime by making deliveries. At night I hide here, with the door barred. The next day I do it again."

"No friends?"

"I have Carra." She could see the white curve of the gharial's neck peeping out of the box in the corner, her beak tucked under her newly healed wing. It wouldn't be long before Carra was gone, too.

His hand stilled. "Who cares for you? Surely you have parents, siblings?"

Her throat tightened, but she didn't let her fingers stop their wandering. He couldn't know the pain it caused her to think about her family. She had to keep it locked tight in her chest, where it could do no more harm. "I have no one."

"You have me." His forefinger nudged beneath her chin, raising it so his gaze could meet hers. "I am yours now."

She gave him a smile without any bitterness because all she could taste was his sweet intentions. "Until the sun rises."

He clasped her to his chest as he struggled upright on his injured arm. "No, Maja. I asked about your clan because I wanted to know what binds you here. Because I hoped it was nothing and no one. Because I hoped you'd—" He stopped himself from finishing the sentence.

"You hoped what?"

He shook his head, his tusks glinting as they swept from the shadows into a pool of moons-light and back into the dark again. "Now that I scent your grief, I'm sorry I wished it. What happened to them to cause you such pain?"

The question cracked her open like a nut, her shell in pieces on the floor and her heart meaty and exposed to his gentle gaze. Safe with him, she realized. He was strong enough to hear what she had to say. "I never knew my father. My mother raised me and my sister by herself. First renting her womb to the Nightborn, and when it failed her, selling her blood at the feeding parlors. But then she found tzat—or tzat found her. And she couldn't keep up anymore. We lost our apartment. Mimma and I—"

She broke, remembering how she and her sister would huddle together for warmth in their alleyway hiding place while their mother offered her neck to every passing Nightborn. She'd grow paler and paler as they drained her far beyond the legal limit. Her yellowed eyes gleamed like an animal's when she earned enough credits for her next round of tzat. Only if there were credits left over did she buy food.

Mimma grew so thin while they lived on the streets. So thin and so cold. Nothing Maja did kept her sister's teeth from chattering, her lips from turning as blue as a Nightborn's. One particularly frigid winter evening, suspecting Mimma might not make it through another night, Maja begged her mother to pay for a room, just this once. To buy food instead of tzat for one day, that's all.

Her mother took them both by the hand and led them swiftly through the streets. But not to a rooming house. To the night market, where she sold Mimma to a stern-looking Nightborn with silver eyes for a hundred credits. When Maja screamed and cried to get her back, her mother had been furious.

"Shut your mouth," she'd hissed, holding Maja's wrist so tightly it burned as she yanked her through the maze of market stalls. "Mimma will be warm and fed. Isn't that what you want for her?"

It was. But not like that.

"It should have been me. You should have sold me," Maja had whispered, a heavy chain of guilt circling her neck and weighing it down. Mimma must be terrified. Who knew what awful plans the hard-faced Nightborn had for a fragile child like her?

"Don't be selfish!" Her mother's hand flashed out and slapped her cheek, leaving a stinging welt behind. As though Maja had made the wish so she'd be the one warm and fed and not to spare Mimma whatever life awaited her, alone and at the mercy of those bloodsuckers! Over the following weeks and months, Maja earned another slap every time she spoke her sister's name, until she stopped mentioning her at all.

"Mimma is your only sibling?" Patrek asked, drawing her mercifully back to the present.

She nodded, willing herself to relax the fists that had tightened at the dark memories. "Sold when she was five summers and I was eight. I don't know what happened to her. My mother bloodwed a Nightborn not long after and left me to fend for myself. He keeps her in tzat and that's all she cares about. I haven't spoken to her in years."

She felt a growl rattle inside the cage of Patrek's ribs. "We'll find her. Your sister. I swear it."

He was good and kind. She already knew that. She let her hand stroke down the planes of his chest, like she was the one comforting him and not the reverse. "I've looked. Everywhere I go, I look for her. I don't think she's in the city anymore. I did a DNA search through the blood parlors, and nothing." It had cost her months of savings, but there was no trace of Mimma in their records. She was gone away—or dead. Or both. A lot could have happened in the twenty summers since then.

"Come with me, Maja," Patrek said suddenly. "Come with me to the mountains."

Her heart stuttered. "What are you asking?"

"You'll be safe in the sanctuary there. There are no Nightborn, no cruel humans, no one to harm you. You could work with the creatures, help them like you helped Carra. You could thrive there." There was a desperate note in his voice that gave her pause. Was it pity?

"You're offering me a job?" She couldn't deny the thought of living in the wildlands, away from the city streets and all the sordid memories that lined them, was appealing. If she had the means to support herself, an escape to the mountains might be more than just a fantasy.

"If you want one. But you could also just live there, free to do as you please. I would provide for you. Protect you as long as you wished me to." He cupped both hands around her like a cage, but rather than feeling trapped by it, she felt secure, like a treasure in a locked chest. If he wanted to rescue her and set her free like one of his wild creatures, then she didn't mind being thought of that way, not by him.

She opened her mouth to say yes, but then remembered what he'd said, that there were no other humans at the mountain sanctuary. There had to be a reason for that. "The other Skarr will welcome my presence? They wouldn't be...angry to have a human in their midst?"

His breath gusted out, warming her. "Some might. But they will accept it when they learn who you are. Who you are *to me*," he amended. His nostrils flared.

He was smelling her again, she could tell, and now she knew just how much he could glean from a scent. He was inhaling their whole night together, from the moment they met until now, the events left in layers on her skin like the rings of a tree. A record of the real things that had happened between them.

Sweat and fear. Salt and blood. Desire and oil, seed and slick. It hadn't *all* been a dream. It hadn't *all* been pretend. An unfamiliar emotion sprouted in her chest. The most dangerous of all.

Hope.

"Who *am* I to you?" She hardly dared to speak the question aloud, but it was more terrifying not knowing and allowing this hope to grow and take root.

"My mate," Patrek said hollowly, pressing one hand to the center of his chest like it pained him. No, it wasn't emptiness in his voice. It was *hunger*.

Did this magnificent, honorable, kind giant want *her*? He'd called her his mate before, when they were pretending, but could it be true? No—he had to be repulsed by the idea of mating with the species that had spelled the demise of his kind. Especially one so much weaker and smaller who would never be able to take his body into hers and give him the pleasure he deserved.

"Surely you don't want a human mate," she stammered, heat rising all over her body.

"I don't," he agreed, deflating her momentarily. But he barreled on, not giving her a chance to mourn. "I want *you*. Skarr instincts only ignite for one female and mine chose *you*. I will always want you, Maja, as long as I live. Please, come to the mountains. Let me care for you there. Keep you from harm. You need not live with me, but I will at least have the satisfaction of knowing that you are safe and fed and have everything you desire. If, by the light of the twins, you do want to nest with me and wear my scent, I would be blessed and honored to call you my mate. To pleasure you in every way I can. To find happiness in your happiness as long as we both live."

She reeled. A lifetime with Patrek? How could he offer this after knowing her a matter of hours? And yet...nothing pricked at her sense of self-preservation. Nothing warned her away. It wasn't crazy. Accepting Patrek felt less risky than walking down the street in the Salt District, something she did every day.

She stood up in his palm so she could look him in the eyes and be sure of him. She grasped his tusks with both hands to steady herself. Fresh arousal pooled between her thighs as she remembered him pinning her to the wall with them. Riding his tongue. She could have that every night. "Are you sure I'd be...enough for you? You can't do all those things you said before."

"That's your only objection? If I swore you were enough for me, then you would agree? You would mate a monster?" His eyes looked unnaturally bright at this close distance.

"Not a monster. But I would mate *you*." Bracing on his tusks, she leaned to brush a kiss against the center of his wide mouth.

When she pulled back to gauge his reaction, his eyes were closed and he sucked in breath after breath of her, tickling her with every exhale. Then his tongue flicked out, and he licked her from ankle bone to eyebrows. She writhed and giggled, and he did it again. Suddenly she was on the floor, cradled in his hand with her legs kicked across his forearm, lost in his enormous shadow as he loomed over her. He bent his head and his wicked tongue found and explored every part of her, from her knobby knees to the dip behind her earlobe to the crevice of her ass.

"What are you doing?!" she gasped when she could catch her breath.

His grin was wide and mischievous. "I promised I'd clean my mate with my tongue, didn't I? Taste our sweetness together?"

"If I were Skarr," she reminded him. "You also said you'd rut me, and that can't happen."

He lipped her whole foot into his mouth and held it between his teeth. Around it, in the naughtiest way, he drawled, "Oh, I think between the two of us, we can find a way."

Chapter 10

PATREKILGAR

He had never spent sweeter hours than the ones watching Maja sleep on his chest, curled up and snoring like a djumjum. The joy of her acceptance spread over him like butter melting on the flesh of a roasted carra root, soaking into his fibers, richening his blood.

His eyes roamed the water-stained ceiling as his thoughts roamed the forests, imagining their life ahead. Foraging for fruit together, making their nest. Staying in it all day and night and finding new ways that their bodies fit together. He'd make his den comfortable for Maja, dig her a pool for bathing and finish the snug side passages to house the injured wildlife she'd surely take in to nurture back to health.

For such a tiny species, she had a huge heart. She was intelligent, too, and brave. Nearly fearless when she'd met him—fearless in the face of a Skarr! And so open and kind, so trusting of him despite all she'd been through. So worshipful of his brutish body. Corek, he was lucky to find his mate.

His mate. His *mate*. He still couldn't believe it.

But when the light of day pierced the tiny room and the gharial rose from her box, stretching her legs and wings with one beady eye always on Patrek, he was faced with a bitter reality. They still had to escape the city, and it wouldn't be easy.

He stroked Maja's cheek with the tip of his thumb until she blinked awake, a smile spreading over her face like the dawn when her eyes finally focused on him.

"You're really here," she murmured, nuzzling into his plates. "I was afraid I dreamed you. It happened, though, didn't it? All of it? I didn't make it up?"

"No," he chuckled, and then laughed again when she clambered up to pepper his face with tiny, fluttering kisses. When they deepened and she sighed against his mouth, her fresh arousal invading his nostrils and addling his thoughts, he had to pull back with a groan. "I wish. But we have some less pleasant tasks to complete while the day lasts."

Maja nodded and slid down to the floor. She pulled on her discarded nightshift and asked, "Are you hungry?"

His guts rumbled to answer her question, and she brightened, producing a half-empty box of cheap ration bars from the cupboard. He could smell their vile manufactured proteins through the wrappers. Patrek shook his head as he pulled up his trousers and banished his already unmanageable cock inside them. "I can't digest those, unfortunately."

Something like shame washed her face as she opened one for herself. "Carra can't either. I'll get you something better when I go out to the butcher for her. What do you like to eat?"

"Most plant foods are agreeable, but don't trouble yourself. Skarr biology is such that we can go some time without food. How often do you eat?"

He should know these things, if he was going to be a good mate to her.

"Once or twice a day at least." She made a face as she chewed her bar. He would find her food she truly liked, food they could share. Through a mouthful, she asked, "I know where to get carra roots—do Skarr eat those?"

"They're a staple of our diet, especially when fruit is scarce."

She gave a decisive nod. "Good. I'll bring you some. You'll need your strength to get us out of the city," she added, before he could voice the protest that was rising in his throat. He didn't want her out there, at risk, without him. His instincts snarled at being stuck in the room while she endangered herself, but what could he do? She was right. He needed fuel for what lay ahead, and she had to go out anyway.

When she asked him how much to buy, he named a figure roughly half the truth, estimating she could only carry that much, and still her eyes went wide. "But less is fine, too," he assured her, and she relaxed. She finished her nasty ration bar and washed her hands, drinking from the faucet before filling a cooking pot with water for him.

He accepted it gratefully, finding that he was parched after the previous night's exertions. "You should wash the rest of you, too," he said between gulps. "As much as I hate for you to be free of my scent, I think even a human could smell that you're covered in my spend."

Maja flushed a pretty shade of rose and scuttled to the wash closet.

"You weren't so shy in the moons-light," he teased her through the door. When she emerged, damp and still blushing, clothed in a fresh jumpsuit that disguised her lovely curves, he was gratified that he could still smell himself on her, if only faintly. Too faint for a Nightborn or human nose, he hoped, but any Skarr would know instantly. He *wanted* them to know that she was under his protection. That she was his—or he was hers. It was the same thing.

She circled him to retrieve and check her datacom. Her flush faded and her face grew drawn when she scanned the screen. "The Authority have set a reward for your capture," she said, lifting her gaze to meet his.

"I thought they might." He'd already been turning over a plan in his head before he woke her. "They're only looking for me, though. So traveling together will actually avoid undue attention. We'll pretend you're a Council wife and I'm your guard, and we'll be able to cross a few districts without being noticed."

She looked down at her plain, worn garment. "No one will believe that."

"They will if they have other things to think about, and my Skarr contacts will provide a distraction. I have a way to contact them. You'll have to buy some things while you're out, clothes for us, and rent a transport, but the credits in your account should cover it. Especially if you stiff your landlord, which you should. This is a storage closet, not an apartment, and it's criminal that he's charging rent for it."

He was rewarded with a smile so sustaining, he might never need to eat another carra root. Patrek gave her the instructions for getting a message to the Skarr network, and reluctantly bid her goodbye.

"I'll be back as soon as I can," she said on her way out, stowing her datacom into one of her jumpsuit's deep pockets. "Bar the door after I leave, just in case."

He huffed out a disbelieving breath when she was gone. *She* was worried about *him*. What did she think would happen while he was stuffed in the basement like extra furnace fuel? She was the one tasked with all the dangerous parts, delivering secret messages and buying contraband and, Manna save him, hauling sacks of carra roots to feed his saltlicking stomach.

He dropped the bar across the door anyway, hoping to please her by completing this tiny task. Now he had hours to wait. Hours to wonder. And nothing to do. At least he had Carra for company.

The gharial clicked her beak at him, mincing across the floor toward his toes, eyeing them like they were mollusks needing their shells cracked. He tucked them under his bulk so she didn't eat them right off his feet and clicked back at her. When she tossed her head, returning his friendly intentions, he reached out to her.

"Let's see that wing of yours."

He could feel where her muscles had wasted slightly during her recovery, but the bone was strong, and she didn't seem too sore. She let him stretch and manipulate her and then, when he'd finished his brief examination, she demonstrated her own exercise routine. If she'd been doing it this diligently

when Maja was gone, it was no surprise she was almost ready for release.

"Such a pretty bird. So smart and so strong," he
praised, a glow in his chest for what Maja had done.
Saved this beautiful creature, given her a home, paid
for proper veterinary treatment when she had no
credits to spare, supported her excellent recovery. It
was a wonder.

The gharial ducked her head again, trilling softly,
and stretched her spindly legs to perch on his knee.
With a sharp look that dared him to object, she settled
there, fluffing her feathers and preening her tail, to
rest.

"I suppose you're coming with us," he said,
amused, but Carra just stuck her head under her
wing and ignored him. He hadn't accounted for her
in his hastily conceived escape plan, but of course, he
should have. At least the question gave him something to do.

He marked the hours by the movement of the
sunlight on the floor, the seconds by the rise and fall
of the gharial's breaths. And he tried to be patient
as a mountain. Maja had errands all over the city to
complete, and that took time. But when the light

started to fade, restlessness invaded his thoughts, and he moved Carra to her box so he could fret without disrupting her.

He drummed his fingers on his plates, picturing Maja as she hurried through the streets, lugging his blasted heavy roots and trying to make it home before the sun slipped away. *Drop them*, he wanted to shout at her. *Run while you still have the light.*

She was almost here. She *had* to be. He waited. And waited. And scratched at the edges of his plates where they ground together. The light pinkened, then grayed, then slipped away, and he wanted to roar as the danger rang in his ears.

The Nightborn were waking. Now he wished she still wore his scent. The scent of Skarr would make them hesitate, even if it didn't stop them. If they hunted her, if they dared to lay a single claw upon her, let alone a fang, he would track them down and snap their necks. He would crush them.

Finally, Maja's steps in the hall. He opened his mouth to greet her, but before he could get a word out, Carra bit him viciously on the soft skin of his wrist, drawing blood. It was lucky she warned him, too, because he was then immediately swamped with the smell of Nightborn. One he recognized—her landlord from the night before. Xakov.

The pounding on the door rattled the whole apartment. "Still no payment in my account, feedbag," Xakov called through the door.

Patrek held his breath, hoping his scent didn't give him away. Surely, if Xakov hadn't detected the gharial after all these weeks, he couldn't sniff out a Skarr inside the apartment, either. The door rattled on its hinges.

"I know you're in there," Xakov continued. "Your time is running out. Manna-moon ends tomorrow. And that's it! No more extensions. No more chances."

Patrek's teeth bared in a fierce grin. They'd be long gone by the time the Nightborn woke tomorrow. But he swallowed the smile as soon as he heard a key slip into the lock. The sneaky bloodsucker was coming in!

Patrek wasn't concerned for his own safety. He had no problem killing the bastard. In fact, he relished the idea of Xakov's surprise when he saw the tiny apartment crammed full of angry Skarr instead of sweet little Maja. He relished the thought of crush-

ing the Nightborn's skull between two fingers like a
brindleberry, retribution for torturing her with con-
stant threats of eviction, her worst fear. But he did
not relish the accompanying image of Maja returning
home to the scene of yet another crime by his hands.
He'd have to use less lethal methods to get rid of
Xakov. He just wasn't sure what that might entail.

Lucky for him, the security bar stopped the door
from opening even a crack. Maja had been right to
worry over him, and he was glad he'd done as his
clever mate asked.

Out in the hall, Xakov cursed both moons and
yelled at Maja through the door a few times. Beside him in her box, the gharial flapped her wings,
apparently amused by the spectacle. Patrek was less
charmed by the outburst. Maja would return any
minute, and he didn't want Xakov on her case, bul-
lying her for the credits when her arms were full of
incriminating purchases.

Sacks of carra roots! He would never forgive himself for that as long as he lived.

Then a dreadful realization crept in. Once Xakov
spotted Maja, he'd know for sure that Patrek was hiding inside the apartment. The security bar had vir-

tually guaranteed it. If Maja wasn't inside the apartment to close it, that meant someone else was. Even the idiot landlord would put it together. He'd threaten Maja, forcing Patrek to open the door and reveal himself. And then Patrek would kill the Nightborn right in front of her. Again.

He could just do it now and spare her the sight. His fingers itched to lift the security bar and pull the door open. But, remembering her dismay when he'd snapped Vilbo's neck, he stopped himself. Their mate bond was so fresh. He wouldn't do anything that might jeopardize her trust in him unless it was absolutely necessary.

After kicking around in the basement passage far too long, Xakov finally retreated upstairs. But uneasiness still tugged at Patrek's tusks, drying his mouth and firing all his senses. The Nightborn would be back before the night was over. He was certain of it.

Chapter 11

MAJA

Somehow Patrek's protection followed her into the streets even when he couldn't. She felt it like a bubble around her, cushioning her from the sounds and smells of the city as she followed the instructions he'd given her and found her way to the Night District.

She never accepted gigs that took her to the Nightborn neighborhoods, not even during daylight hours, so the way was unfamiliar, but it wasn't hard to spot the enormous Skarr guard blocking the gate in front of one of the large estates. He was even taller and wider than Patrek, his rocky plates lighter and more irregular, but his tusks were sawn short and capped with round finials.

"Blood entrance is on the side," he grunted when she approached, motioning her away. She could tell the moment he caught her scent, because his head snapped toward her, his great nostrils working, his puzzlement written all over his face. "Why do you smell of Skarr, human?"

"Are you Hinrivik?" she asked.

"Who wants to know?" His plates scraped as he shifted to scan the streets for threats. She believed Patrek that Hinrivik was a friend of his, but he didn't seem friendly. He seemed suspicious at best. Hostile at worse.

"I'm supposed to give you this." She held up the folded paper, proud that she kept her hand from trembling as he plucked it from her grip with his massive fingers. "Patrek needs your help."

The huge Skarr didn't even look at the paper, only *her* as he leaned close and sucked in a deep breath that ruffled her hair. "Are you his *pet*?" His tone was scathing, something near disgust. "I knew Patrek was soft, but I didn't think he was that weak. How low the Skarr have sunk."

"I'm his mate," she snapped, anger surging to compete with the flood of joy she felt at saying the words out loud. Patrek wasn't weak. He'd killed for her when it was necessary. He had inner strength, too, so he didn't have to solve every problem with his fists. That was real strength.

Hinrivik's tense posture went completely slack. He gaped at her, no longer looking for outside threats. "How is it possible?"

"Surely you know the mating habits of your kind," she said, blushing to the roots of her hair. She wasn't about to recount the details even though she had played them over in her mind a hundred times during her walk from the Salt District.

"Manna save me, a human," Hinrivik mumbled, shaking his head.

The gentle bubble that had cushioned her from the saltlicking reality of her situation popped. Tears pricked her eyes, but she forced herself to keep her composure. A union between a Skarr and a human was unheard of, so Hinrivik's reaction was natural. His personal feelings about their mating didn't factor, as long as he helped Patrek. "He said you could provide a distraction so we can get out of the city. The details are on the paper. Will you do it?"

Hinrivik was still staring down at her like he was lost. "You accepted his claim? You weren't afraid or...repulsed?" There was something vulnerable behind his craggy plates.

"No."

His brow ridges rippled as he rubbed the brass tips of his tusks and looked at her like he was trying to decide which cut of meat to buy at the butcher's. Though Skarr didn't eat meat, of course. Patrek said they liked plant foods.

"Are you typical of your kind?" Once the words were out of his mouth, Hinrivik seemed embarrassed to have asked the question. "I mean, are there other females who don't fear us?"

"I don't know," she answered kindly. She could guess what he was feeling. That seductive seed of hope that she'd let grow and bloom last night was sprouting in him, too, and she wouldn't crush it. "Most women my age are already matched or contracted. But some aren't, and I think it's possible that one would come to love you if she got to know you."

Hinrivik straightened and scanned up and down the street, seeming to have remembered his guard duties. Then he glanced at the paper to see what Patrek had written. "I'll do this for your mate," he said gruffly, refolding it and tucking it into his pocket. "And I have an extra uniform in the guard house if that might help."

Maja let out a relieved breath. "It will, thank you."

She took the heavy sack of clothing he brought out and hurried to complete the rest of her errands. She crossed two districts to rent a luxury transport in person to avoid a transaction record in her datacom, then parked it in a neighborhood where it wouldn't stand out. She purchased herself a fancy dress and long cloak that cost more than all the rest of her clothes put together. The line at the butcher shop took forever, and by the time she reached the car-ra-root warehouse, weighed down by her purchases, it was closed, the door barred and shutters locked over the windows.

She knocked anyway, and the vendor, a sandy-haired man she recognized from delivery gigs, cracked open the door.

He narrowed his pale eyes at her. "Maja, right? You shouldn't be out."

"It's an hour until the Nightborn wake," she said, annoyed by his condescending tone. "Since when do you close before the sun goes down?"

He blinked at her. "Is your com broken? There's a rogue Skarr on the loose. Murdered something like three guys since yesterday. Council stopped sales on carra root to try and flush the monster out. Now I'm stuck with a warehouse full of the stuff and nobody can buy it."

She rolled her eyes. Funny how one dead Nightborn could turn into three humans, just like that. "I need a couple sacks, if you have them. I'll pay twice the usual."

He sighed heavily, glancing over his shoulder at the contents of the warehouse behind him. "Fine. Don't tell anyone where you got it. And don't blame me if it draws the killer right to you. I won't cry if I read about you in tomorrow's alerts."

The roots were heavy, but no heavier than her usual deliveries. She wished the sun wasn't so low in the sky, though. She had just enough time to make it back, but only if she hurried. Loaded down, she

headed toward home, taking every shortcut she knew
as the daylight gave way to twilight and then true
night.

The Nightborn were waking. She shivered, feeling
the prickle of her prey instincts waking along with
them, and quickened her steps.

This would be the last time she'd make this dash.
Tomorrow, she and Patrek would be somewhere up
the coastline. She just had to make it home. The
thought of seeing him again made her bags feel lighter
despite the cold sweat slipping down her back. Only
a few blocks more, and she'd be in his arms.

A squad of Council enforcers, who policed during
the daylight hours and handled human-on-human
crime, blocked the alleyway that led into the Salt
District and were searching bags and datacoms. She
reversed course to take an alternate route. But that
way was blocked, too.

"What's going on?" she asked an older woman
with tzat-yellowed eyes who was watching the com-
motion.

"Looking for some girl. A thief. There's a reward."
The woman squinted at her suspiciously, and a dull
punch of fear hit Maja in the guts.

She moved a distance away and ducked into an alcove to check her datacom. Her own face stared back at her from the most recent alert. An old picture, thank Corek, from back when her hair was long and braided and she had fuller cheeks. Wanted for stealing art from a Council estate.

Clearly a bogus charge to cover up for what really happened, but it meant that somehow, someone powerful had connected her to the impran's release. Pulled strings to get the Council enforcers on the hunt for her.

How, though? She couldn't have left much evidence inside the stone building. She had the djumjum suit on the whole time, and Patrek had burned it in the incinerator. The only thing she'd touched with her bare hands had been the buckle on the impran's restraints, and as far as she knew, her fingerprints weren't in the Council system, only her DNA from when she'd given a sample to the blood parlor to help find Mimma.

She groaned. Of course, that's how they knew who she was. In her panic to free the impran, she'd stripped off the djumjum paws and dropped them on the floor, and she'd never picked them back up after the alarm went off. Her DNA was probably all over the inside of those gloves.

Manna save her, she was out of options. If a Council member knew she'd released the impran, then he knew she and Patrek were working together, too. They'd search her apartment soon. She had to warn Patrek so he and Carra could get out.

She threw her datacom in a trash can and dropped the bags of carra roots so she could move more quickly as she tried to blend with the other humans on the streets. More were out than usual to see what the fuss was about, so she clung to one small group and then another like she had in the djumjum herd. Patrek would laugh to hear she'd picked up tips from her time in the disguise, and the thought of his warm, rolling chuckle kept her panic at bay.

But every street she tried was blocked by Council enforcers canvassing for her, Authority wheeling in the sky above, or both.

What could she do? Eyes were following her on the streets as she exhausted all routes to G-block, and when she doubled back, she could practically hear people wondering *is that her* as she passed by them again. Even without the sacks of carra root, she was too recognizable with all these bags. Might as well get rid of them; the plan was ruined anyway.

She'd made so many mistakes. Wrecked so many plans.

In the shadow of a building, Maja shed her jumpsuit like a skin and pulled her beautiful Council-wife clothes on. The cloak's hood would help make her less recognizable, plus she couldn't bear to throw them away. She tucked the butcher's packet in the cloak's deep pocket, pausing on a bridge over a sludgy irrigation ditch to dump the heavy Skarr uniform. She murmured a low apology to Hinrivik for wasting his sacrifice as she did so, but it was better to lose the uniform than have him tied to their failed escape attempt.

Then she turned her back on the Salt District and walked away. The only place she could think to go was where the transport was parked on the edge of the next district. She could hide in the vehicle until the sun rose, and then drive it out of the city on her own at first light when the Nightborn went to sleep again.

The hood hid the tears that slipped down her cheeks when she thought of Patrek waiting for her.

Worrying about her. The Council enforcers and Authority would be at the apartment soon, if they weren't there already. It might take some time for them to breach the door. They'd have to blast it with explosives, likely killing him and Carra, too.

She'd never see either of them again. She dragged herself through the streets, for once not even conscious of the Nightborn who passed overhead, their dark wings shuttering out the stars.

Even if Patrek managed to fight his way out and survived, why would he want to reunite with her, the stupid human who'd convinced him to hole up in a storage closet instead of running to the mountains where he'd be safe? The stupid human who'd forced him to kill for her, who ruined his noble plans to save countless animals, who'd left evidence at the scene of a crime that he hadn't asked her to commit. The stupid human who'd believed for a night that she deserved to be his mate.

She couldn't let the Authority get their claws on him. Maybe if she turned herself in, the distraction would allow Patrek the time he needed to escape? But last time she'd tried that, she'd just made everything worse! Blinded by her tears, Maja stumbled over a curb and threw her arms out to break her fall.

But she never hit the ground.

A huge pair of hands caught and cradled her, and a sound that spoke to her soul rattled through her. Calming her. Alleviating the deep guilt and shame that had permeated her body.

Patrek.

"How?" she asked, when he quieted his coo and she could speak again. "How did you get out? How did you find me?"

"I told you I could find you in the deepest forest," he said, grinning like a fool.

Chapter 12

PATREKILGAR

Maja gaped at him. "You found me by my scent?"

His smile stretched so wide, he thought it might push the tusks off his face. "That, and the tracker. It's still glued to your tooth, thank Corek. I had the receiver in my rucksack." He flashed the small device at her.

He'd found the receiver when he was emptying his rucksack to make room for the gharial. He'd decided to smuggle her out rather than sit in the basement waiting for Xakov to come back with the Authority in tow. And it was a good thing he had, too—the streets of the Salt District had been teeming with Council enforcers. They were so busy looking for Maja that nobody stopped him. He'd just walked right out.

Well, he had to crack a few heads together. But he didn't kill anyone.

"Carra is with me," he added, shifting so she could see the pack on his back. "I thought we could release her on the way to the sanctuary. Were you able to find everything we needed?"

"I had to drop your carra roots to get away," she said, looking up at him with eyes that welled with tears. "I'm so sorry. You must be starving."

Sweet mate. Her hood fell back, and he kissed the top of her head. "I'm fine. Night Mother, I'm happy you're safe. I wish you'd never been in danger at all. That was my failing."

"I had to throw away the uniform Hinrivik gave me," she hiccuped, and a desolate wreath of fear-smell circled her. "I ruined your plan *again*."

"You gave him the message?" She nodded. That was good news. Very good news. He stroked her back through the soft folds of her blue velvet cloak. "And you got new clothes, I see."

"The transport, too. I left it on Chalnea Lane near the park," she offered shyly. That was only a few blocks ahead. Good thing, too, because he could smell Nightborn coming—a lot of them, judging by the gusts of scent that hit him.

"See? You haven't ruined anything. You did so well, Maja." Patrek beamed down at her as he tucked her against his chest and began walking swiftly toward the intersection she'd mentioned. He felt her tiny body relax against him, and the sense of rightness at having her in his arms was almost overwhelming. He'd never let her go again. "My perfect mate."

He pressed his nose to her head fur and breathed her in, seeking the traces of his scent beneath her fear. There it was, a steady, undeniable background. He couldn't wait to wash away the sourness of the day now that they were reunited. But it would have to wait until they left the dangers of the city.

He located the transport exactly where Maja said it would be and was gratified that she'd chosen a quiet street in the wealthy Council District. The Authority patrols were sparse here, and the humans were all inside for the night. With any luck, the transport wouldn't be stopped before they reached the city boundary. But to be safe, he left the gharial in his rucksack.

They were almost to the edge of the final district when they were stopped at a checkpoint, by a skinny, pimpled enforcer who looked barely old enough to wear the uniform. "I-identification?" he stammered when Patrek opened the transport window.

"Council business," he grunted, jerking his head toward Maja with her plush hood pulled up to hide her face. He hoped the nervous human would wave them through instead of noticing that Patrek wasn't wearing an estate's uniform.

But no. The enforcer's nerves turned into officiousness. "I'll need to run your credentials."

"My credentials." Patrek's face plates ground as he glowered. "Do you doubt that I'm the Skarr guard of a Council member?"

"N-no, but—"

"Shall I get out of the transport so you can be *sure*?"

The enforcer took two steps back. "That's not necessary, just—"

Patrek reached out and grasped the man's tunic and jerked him close. "Maybe you want to com my employer? Wake him up and tell him you're delaying his wife's return during the riskiest hour of the night?"

The unpleasant scent of the enforcer's nerves was suddenly overwhelmed by the acrid smell of ammonia. A wet spot spread across the front of his trousers. He choked out, "Go on ahead, sir. Have a good night."

Patrek snorted and dropped the man, not even sparing him a second look as he closed the window and drove off. He was a little bit sorry that he hadn't had to be more persuasive.

In his peripheral vision, Maja shook her head. "I love it when you do that."

"Do what?" he asked, keeping his eyes on the road ahead. The sea appeared, flickering between buildings on the right. Soon they'd emerge onto the winding coastal highway that was bracketed between the fierce, salty waves and the wildlands. The first step on the path to freedom, since Council enforcers wouldn't patrol beyond the city boundary.

"That enforcer could have ruined my life. Touched me, made me do things. Hurt me. Locked me up forever. My whole life, I've been at the mercy of men like him. But he couldn't do that because you were with me. You didn't even have to say much. Just your presence kept me safe. All you had to do was exist." Her words were happy, but her scent was tinged with sadness, so he waited for her to unburden her heart. Finally she said, "Are you sure you want me with you in the mountains? What if the other Skarr don't accept me? Hinrivik seemed disgusted by the thought of us together."

Patrek chuckled. "Don't mind him. He's just jealous. He's been in love with the human he guards for years. The mountain Skarr will accept you because they'll have no other choice. You're my mate; it's simply the truth."

Maja sighed. "I wish I brought as much to your life as you do to mine. I'm grateful for your care, though, even if it comes from pity."

He switched the transport to autopilot as they left the city behind and turned toward her, drawing her onto his lap. "Manna save us, I don't pity you. If anything, you should pity me, because of how desperately I need you."

Her eyes welled as she curled into his belly. "But how can I satisfy you, truly?"

He growled at her fear-scent. "You do. Never doubt it. You satisfy the animal in me. The one that was always restless and hungry until it caught your scent."

"You're satisfied because I smell good?" She giggled through a yawn, sounding slightly drunk on her exhaustion.

"Mmm," he murmured his agreement against the top of her head, pulling fresh draughts of her into his lungs. "You smell so sweet. You taste so sweet."

She *bloomed* at his words, and her contented sigh was so pretty that he wished he could forge it into rings to wear on his tusks every day. She snuggled deeper into his lap, pressing into his ravenous cock. It swelled and pulsed at her touch, imploring for more. As if he could ask that of her after her grueling day! In a transport, too. She deserved so much better. She deserved fruit and furs and a full night of rest, at the very least.

"Don't listen to him," he said, chuckling ruefully. He squeezed his hand between her and his mindless beast, but Maja pushed his fingers away until he relented.

"I like him," she insisted. She turned her face to nuzzle against his cock, wrapping her arms around his shaft through his trousers and cuddling it like a beloved, naughty pet. Well, perhaps it was her pet, tamed and at her command.

"Sleep now," he said to her, caressing the soft strands of her head fur. The texture reminded him of the verdant moss that grew near his den—the one that would soon be her den, too, he realized with a jolt. Humans lived in mated pairs, not separate as the Skarr did. It would be *their* den, where they'd nest and mate for the rest of their days on Salaan.

His cock wanted to howl at the thought. Apparently, it wasn't tamed quite yet. Maja seemed eager to take on that challenge, though, and he would let her try as many times as she liked. "Rest, because you'll need your strength for what's to come, little mate. I'll watch over you, and I'll be here when you wake."

He felt the last bit of her tension drain away as she melted into sleep. He used the quiet hours before dawn to feed the gharial the packet of djumjum meat that Maja had tucked into her cloak pocket, and when the sun warmed the surface of the sea, and he was certain that the Authority had abandoned their pursuit, he directed the transport to pull over beside a rocky promontory that overlooked the water.

Cradling Maja as gently as he could so she wouldn't wake, he swung the gharial's rucksack onto his back and scaled the rocks, pleased that his injured shoulder hardly protested as he made the climb. When he reached the top, the sun had fully risen, and warm salty winds whipped up the cliffs to welcome them. Maja opened her eyes and gasped when she saw the view that stretched out in every direction.

The sea on one side, the forests another. In the distance, the mountains they'd call home. And behind them, the way they'd come, the city was too small to see, although a smudge of smoke marred the area above where he knew it lay.

His little distraction, courtesy of Hinrivik. Though too late to aid their escape, the explosion would keep the Council enforcers and Authority busy for some time. He couldn't suppress his grin as he set Maja gently down.

"I've never seen so much sky," she said wondering-ly, her face turned up so the golden sunlight made her skin glow. "Is it like this where you live? So...open?"

"Where *we* live," he corrected, opening the pack so Carra could step out onto the rocks, too. The gharial flexed her wings, flapping into the wind as she stretched her legs and neck. "On the top of the peaks, it's even more wide and wild. You can see forever. I'll take you there sometime."

"I'd like that." Maja reached up a shy hand and grasped his little finger, and the gesture made his heart feel like it'd spread its wings.

Carra, who'd been staring out at the vast ocean, stepped in front of them and dipped her head low in front of Maja, clacking her bill in a syncopated rhythm. Maja looked puzzled as she stroked the ghar-ial's neck with her free hand. "She's never done this before. I can't tell what she wants."

"She's asking your permission," Patrek said gently. "The way gharial mates do when one leaves the other on the nest."

"Oh. *Oh.*" She blinked, looking out at the sun-tipped waves. He could smell sorrow muddling her sweetness. "Yes. Go, Carra. You don't need my permission to be free."

With one last preen of Maja's head fur, the gharial launched from the rock, gliding down to kiss the surface of the sea before wheeling in a huge arc, like she was showing off for them. Then she beat her wings with powerful strokes, propelling herself toward the horizon.

Maja squeezed his finger as the last glimpse of Carra's white tail feathers became a speck of light and then vanished, and when Patrek looked down at her, she had tears streaming down her cheeks. He'd missed the scent because it was so like the ocean's. He couldn't help it; he took her in his arms and cooed for her, feeling her grief like an ache in the center of his chest. He knew loss, too. He knew loneliness. When he let the sound wane, she offered him a tremulous smile.

"I'm not sad, I swear. I'm happy she's whole and free. I'll miss her company, but that's not enough reason to keep her with me, is it?"

Little thief. Her words stole the breath from his lungs. Was that what he was doing? Keeping Maja for his own comfort and companionship when she should be free? With the tip of his forefinger, he touched her plush lips and traced the line of her jaw.

"When we get to the mountains, I won't hold you to our agreement," he said. "You know that, don't you?"

Her brown eyes narrowed—not fragile glasswing beetles after all, but the glowing coals of an incinerator. "What does that mean? What are you saying, Patrek? You changed your mind about us?"

Something desperate rose in him until his whole skin felt wrong. "No, not at all. But you can walk away any time, sweet Maja. It will rip out my heart, but I won't trap you. Any time you tire of me, you can have...*more*." He made a stupid gesture at the sea, like he was suggesting she take flight like the gharial.

"Lift me up so I can look you in the eye," she commanded, still spitting sparks at him. When they were eye-to-eye, she took hold of his tusks. Her nearness perfumed the air, and he couldn't help breathing her in, searching for his scent mixed with hers. "That's right, get a good sniff. Maybe it will remind you that I'm your *mate*, you big thick mountain. You've saved my life at least five times in the last two days. You're the kindest person I've ever met, and your tongue has touched parts of me I didn't know brought pleasure until you wrung it out of me. Night Mother knows, I'll be clinging to your giant cock like a suffocating sea star until the day I die. Just try and get rid of me."

She looked so defiant, exactly as she had when she'd refused to get out of his pants, that he barked a laugh. Sweet, stubborn mate. He was foolish to think that she'd ever do anything she didn't want to do.

He flicked his tongue out to tease under her fancy new skirts and make her squeal. "I like these new clothes," he said, rejoicing in the salt and sweet of her. "But you don't taste nearly enough like me."

Maja set her mouth in a prim line. "Then I guess we should do something about that."

Chapter 13

MAJA

Gripping Patrek's slippery cock between her knees, bare and glistening in the sunlight with his oils, riding a mountain on top of a mountain, Maja had never felt more free.

She braced her hands and slid over his shaft, exulting at every groan it dragged out of his chest. The texture of his olje was like dozens of fingers prodding her clit, teasing her until it was almost too much. No, not fingers—*tongues*.

"Maja." He said her name with a note of warning, heating her. He was close to spilling, and in that moment, there was nothing she wanted more than to completely unravel him. She could feel the skin under her thighs tighten as he struggled to keep his release at bay, and her core *ached* for him. There was so much strength in his restraint, she couldn't imagine his power when he let go.

"I wish you could fill me," she blurted out, lost in her own desire, lost in the wind that swept up from the sea to plant salty kisses on her face and arms and breasts. "I wish you could rut me and spill inside me."

She felt his hands shift and slide up her body. With one, he cradled her upper back, caressing her hair with his thumb. The other cupped her from behind. He pushed her forward until her chest was sliding against him, his olje licking at her nipples now, too, as he moved her up and down, taking his pleasure from her whole body as he gave her the same.

It was so good, too good. And then something nudged between her thighs, spreading them, hard and insistent against her opening. His little finger, she realized. His smallest part. It was still so big, *too* big, but she wanted it more than anything.

"Like this?" Patrek demanded, pressing it into her, his eyes glittering as bright as the sun on the breakers far below them. She whimpered and raised her hips so he could better the angle and felt the pressure as the tip of his finger begged entrance. "Is this what you wish for?"

"Yes," she breathed. Her folds were so slick and swollen that they should have made its passage easy, but even the barest tip of his finger stretched her to her limits.

"Open for me," he coaxed, the pressure of his finger never waning. It was overwhelming—thick and inexorable and delicious.

"It's too big, though. I can't," she whined impatiently. She wrapped her arms around his cock so he didn't push her right off of it, and his breath hissed out when she squeezed him.

"Sweet mate," he crooned, still grinding his cock against her. "You can. Relax and let me please you."

He cooed then, the deep rumble unlocking her muscles, robbing her of every tension. It eased her body just enough that he could slide his finger home. Her walls fluttered and balked as it sank in deeper and then deeper, filling her with a satisfaction so intense it rivaled any orgasm she'd ever had.

"Good little mate. You're taking me so well." He stroked in and out, pressing on her every nerve, and she thought she might scream if there were any air left in her lungs. "So warm and tight, it's like touching the sunshine, being inside you."

"Patrek," she murmured against his soft skin as he matched his finger to the rhythm of his hands and hips so the sensations all blurred together and he was inside and outside and underneath and on top of her all at once. Her tether to reality thinned and snapped. "I think I might fly away."

"Yes, love, I want you to fly."

Love, he'd called her love! The ceiling of the sky opened up to swallow her and for an exquisite moment it really did feel like flying. And then her pleasure pulled her down, his finger like the crash of waves pounding her into him, giving and taking in equal measure, leaving her boneless and helpless and gasping and glorious.

She wanted to say that she loved him, too, but she was unable to muster her lips and tongue to move as aftershocks still rippled through her.

"I never dreamed," Patrek choked, the tendons in his neck standing out even through his plates. "Maja, I never dreamed."

And he came, flooding them both with an ocean of hot, sweet, sticky seed that washed away any doubts that might have lingered. They stayed still and silent afterward, basking in each other and their freedom. Maja wasn't willing to shatter the moment with words. It was too perfect.

Eventually, he made a face at the mess everywhere and moved to withdraw his finger from her core. She clamped her legs around his hand so he couldn't. "Not yet."

"I'll replace it with my tongue, I promise." He gave her a wicked grin, and she felt his cock startle in her arms at his own suggestion. She kissed it, and he laughed. "Leave your pet and come hang on my tusks so I can taste you."

"I don't want this to end," she said wistfully, taking it all in—the enormity of the sea and sky and rocks and *him*, her feelings for him—and trying to commit it to memory so she'd never lose it.

"It won't end. Don't be afraid. I won't let anyone take it from us."

Regretfully, they couldn't stay on the rock all day. Patrek carried her down the cliffs and then a brief distance along the shoreline until they found a small, private beach. They rinsed off in the salty shallows before resuming their drive.

The time passed quickly in the transport. Maja couldn't get enough of the view, her attention split between the sea, the forests that grew impossibly thicker as they traveled, and the tantalizing glimpses of the mountain peaks ahead. Patrek did his best to keep up with her questions, smiling at her excitement and pointing out landmarks he recognized.

The further they went from the city, the more settled and happy Maja felt, and eventually she relaxed enough to eat a ration bar from the bag and then nap. When she woke, it was to Patrek lifting her from the transport.

"Are we there?" she asked, rubbing her eyes.

His deep laugh rumbled against her. "Not quite. The transport can't take us where we're going. The rest of the way we'll travel on foot. We'll reach it before dark, though."

After they'd both checked to make sure that they'd packed all their possessions in his backpack, Patrek wiped down the interior of the vehicle and pro-grammed it to return to the rental outlet in the city. Even if it were connected with their disappearance, the Authority would never suspect that they hadn't just changed transports and continued on the coastal highway, because the apparent way ahead didn't look like a way at all, Maja thought. It looked like a tumble of boulders.

"I don't think I can climb that in these Council clothes," she said doubtfully, hefting the heavy velvet.

"I don't mind if you take them off. There's no one here to see you." He laughed at her expression and lifted her in his arms again, strolling up the side of the mountain as easily as if the boulders were a set of stairs. "I can't wait to introduce you to the clan as my mate."

The joy in his voice was contagious, and Maja's heart thumped with anticipation as Patrek maneu-vered up and up through the rocky passages marked by stone columns. In his element, unconstrained by streets and architecture not designed for his kind, his strength had an added grace and purpose. He fit perfectly here, just as she fit perfectly in his arms. And the craggy cliffs and even craggier trees that clung to them seemed to embrace her, too. She was confident that she'd love living in this new wilderness with him, among his people.

"See that?" He paused beside a stone column and brushed his fingers over a carved symbol in it, shifting so she could see it better. Three triangular mountains juxtaposed with two moons, one crescent and one full. "Our clan sign. We're nearly home. Don't be alarmed when you see my den. It isn't much right now because I've been away, but I'll make it good for you, Maja. If it's really terrible, we can stay with my brother while I fix it up."

Maja barely sensed a blur in her vision before a stone exploded against the cliff face directly in front of them. Fragments of rock stung her cheeks. She yelped, and Patrek yanked her to his chest, cupping two huge, protective hands around her like a suit of armor.

"Alrek!" he bellowed. "I'd know that terrible aim anywhere. Show yourself!"

She peeked through a gap in Patrek's fingers and saw an enormous Skarr step from behind one of the largest granite boulders ahead.

"I hit where I meant to. What in Salaan's name do you think you're doing?" the new giant growled. He could have been part of the mountain himself, his dark gray plates tinged green at the shoulders as though moss grew there. One tusk curved away from his jaw, long and proud, but the other was brutally splintered and broken. He held another rock in his hands, poised to throw it at them.

"Coming home." Patrek shifted, still holding her close, but moving one hand slightly so she could see better. "This is Maja. Maja, this is Alrek, our clan chief."

"Hello," she squeaked out.

Alrek swept his gaze over her dismissively, returning to Patrek's face as he tossed the rock from hand to hand. "What kind of traitor shows a human our clan sign?"

"I'm no traitor. This is my mate. You can smell her if you don't believe me. She wears my oils."

"I scented her an hour ago, and it turned my stomach," Alrek scoffed. "She's a plaything at best. Not a true mate. Don't delude yourself, brother."

Maja sucked in her breath. This was Patrek's brother? The one they were to stay with? His family?

If the clan chief disapproved of her, it was one thing. If his family disapproved, it was another. But if they were one and the same? She had no hope of acceptance among the Skarr.

She pulled up on Patrek's tusk to whisper in his ear, "Maybe we should just go?"

"Yes, turn around and take your pet back to the city." Of course, he'd overheard her. Those damn Skarr senses. "No brother of mine would bring a human to my door."

Maja felt Patrek sag slightly at those words, and a guilty knot tightened in her belly, thinking of her own sibling. She would do anything to see Mimma again. The thought of Patrek losing his brother over her was almost too much to bear. "We can't go back to the city. The Council is after me and the Authority is after him. You don't have to accept me as his mate, but at least show Patrek some compassion. Night Mother, the Skarr have so little left on Salaan. Don't deprive yourself of each other!"

The mossy giant regarded her for a long moment. Then, to her surprise, he gave a slow nod. "I hear you, female."

"Her name is Maja," Patrek said again, adding stubbornly, "She is my true mate."

"Salaan save us," Alrek grunted, turning to stride away from them. It was clear that he didn't believe it, but at least he was no longer flinging rocks at them.

As Patrek followed his brother up the mountain, Maja put a reassuring hand on his rocky cheek where his tusk met his jaw, swaying slightly with each of his enormous steps. "It doesn't matter what he thinks. Or what anybody thinks. We know the truth."

"Has he hunted you?" came Alrek's sharp question from ahead. He did not turn or slow his pace, so she raised her voice to answer truthfully.

"Yes. He found me by my scent in the city. Hunted me through the streets and saved me."

"Did he gift you and guard you?"

"No," Patrek said swiftly, before Maja could answer that he had, his tone guilt-ridden. "I didn't do it properly. But it's true all the same. My instinct burns for her, and she accepts me and calls me her mate."

"You dishonor her," Alrek barked in a tight voice.

"No!" Maja cried, disbelieving tears thickening her throat as she clung to Patrek. "He has done nothing but honor me. With his words and his care and his body, too."

Alrek whirled on them, his chastising tone as searing as a forest fire as he stabbed his forefinger, as thick as her leg, straight at her. "I have no doubt he used you. But he did not gift you. He did not ensure your peaceful rest."

"He did," she sobbed. "You did," she insisted, when Patrek shook his heavy head, his tusks cutting the air above her. "You guarded me all night. I've never slept so well as on your chest."

"I did not gift you, my sweet Maja. You did not eat." He sounded miserable even as he held her close. Was he really trying to deny her now that they were with his clan? Her stomach wobbled, and then she remembered.

"I ate the djumjum treat! When I was in the building with the impran. I wouldn't have had that without you."

A bitter laugh burst out of him as he raised his eyes to the sky. "That only proves how I've failed you. My brother is right, I have dishonored you."

"Stop saying that," Maja begged him, tears still pouring down her cheeks, seeping between her lips until she tasted salt. Patrek stroked her back, but his gaze was sorrowful.

"The impran's building? Does she mean Josefat's collection?" Alrek *growled* the question, and the sound was so beastlike that it raised the tiny hairs on the back of Maja's neck. "You sent a *female* into his clutches?"

Patrek winced with his whole body. "I did."

Why was Alrek looking at him with disgust twisting his rugged features until they resembled a pile of rubble? Patrek had been nothing but honorable toward her. Had even *refused* her at first. She'd convinced him to let her do the work and then messed up the whole operation, and he'd still paid her, still made sure she got home safely. "He didn't want to let me, but I insisted." She tried to keep the tremble out of her voice as she added, "I needed the money."

A grating noise of disgust came from Alrek. "Of course. That's all humans care about, isn't it? Salaan swallow the rest of us, as long as the humans have their precious credits."

Maja glanced up at Patrek and her stomach hollowed at how his stony brow furrowed, his jaw tight as he faced off against his brother. She should not have come. Should not be standing between siblings, fracturing their family with her mere presence. She could still go back to the transport. She opened her mouth to say so, but Patrek spoke first.

"She needed it for her gharial," he said, his voice blazing like midday sun, warming her with his anger. Even if coming to the mountains was a mistake, he did not regret her. He was not ashamed. At least that was clear. "She saved one when it was shot at the docks, Alrek. Gave it food from her own mouth to help it recover, paid for medicine she couldn't afford. She would have been turned out of her home without those credits, so yes, she needed them. And she knew nothing of our mission at Josefat's, yet when she saw the impran and its condition, rather than do as I asked her and place the tracker, she set it free, knowing she likely wouldn't get paid as a result. She saved it instead of herself. She has the skin of a human, but the heart of a Skarr."

Maja's heart felt nothing but human, beating weak and lopsided at his praise for her, his defense of her. No one in her life had ever stood up for her or risked anything for her, not even her own mother. "I love you," she blurted out, fearing it could be the end,

feeling silly and self-conscious when both mountainous men stilled and stared at her, cupped in Patrek's massive hands.

"She will stay in Brannica's midden," Alrek grunted, drawing both their attention. With that cryptic
statement, he turned his back on them and walked
away.

Chapter 14

PATREKILGAR

It felt like the wind had been knocked out of him, like Alrek had thrown a boulder at his chest and actually hit his target for once. He had a *chance*. A real chance to prove his love for Maja, for them to be fully accepted by the clan, not just tolerated and whispered about.

Buoyed, he hurried after Alrek until he was slapped by a wave of sour bitterness from the tiny, precious mate in his hands. He stopped to draw another breath, disbelieving his own senses. She was...*sad?* How could she be, on what was possibly the best day of his life?

"What troubles you, little heart?" he asked her, stroking her head fur with one finger. She leaned into his touch, and he felt the moisture on her cheeks.

"I want to stay with you, not with this Brannica person. Why can't we stay together? Are you sending me away?" She gripped her lip with her tiny, blunt teeth and tried to scrub away her tears. She might as well have torn a hole in his heart.

"No, never. Brannica is—*was* his mate. The last of our females, the only one whose midden still stands. It is a great honor that Alrek offered it to you for your safety and rest until I fulfill the ritual the right way. It means he is giving you the same consideration as he would a Skarr female. I'm sorry I didn't explain right away. I forgot for a moment that our people and ways aren't familiar to you."

"I want to learn them." She gave him a shaky smile. "How long has she been gone?"

Patrek's neck bent to brush his lips over the top of her head, his skull feeling heavier than it should as he remembered that dark time. "Six years ago. Skarr males break a tusk when their mate dies and only cap it when they have made peace with Salaan. Many broke their tusks when Brannica left us, as she was our last hope. Alrek never capped his. You saw him. He mourns her still."

"I can't blame him," Maja murmured, her tears growing thick again. "That's so sad. I can't imagine what it must have been like for all of you, but especially for him."

He cooed for her, lingering in the circle of trees outside the clan stones until her sour scent sweetened again, not wanting to introduce her when she smelled of despair. But he needn't have worried. When they reached the meadow in the bottom of the ancient caldera that served as the meeting grounds for his kind, it was empty and quiet, save for the babbling brook that threaded through its center. The only observers were the naked fingers of stone that jutted up into the sky all around them. Even Alrek had disappeared, likely into his own den behind a craggy column at the base of the highest peak.

"Welcome home," he said, holding her up so she could see. "This is Skarr's Hand. See the five peaks? They are the Fingers. My den is in that one, called the Thumb. So is Alrek's and a few of our cousins. Families usually den near each other, but we can make ours wherever it pleases you."

Maja pulled up on his tusks to scan the area, sending another helpless tug of affection into his belly that she could use him this way. "Where is everyone?" she asked worriedly.

Patrek's chest swelled. "Another honor. Alrek has warned them that you are here. No unmated male would dare to approach a Skarr female without her permission. They are waiting for your signal. Your acceptance. They are keeping the old ways for you, little heart."

"Oh," she said softly, the noise as bright to his ears as the wildflowers that dotted the Hand's meadow. He desperately hoped she would blossom here, too. "I want to do the same for them. What's the signal?"

"Settle into Brannica's midden and make your nest, and they will know you have judged this place as safe. Then they will show themselves."

She grabbed his thumb and squeezed. "I can do that. As long as we're not apart for too long."

"My brave, beautiful heart," he rumbled as he made his way to the edge of the meadow where the stream cut through the rocks, tumbling over a cliff and down the side of the mountain below in a lacey waterfall that dissolved completely to mist before it hit the bottom. There in the rising spray, framed by ancient addoc trees, Brannica's mossy midden hugged the earth.

He parted the ferns that had grown up to disguise the wooden door and pushed it open, setting Maja down gently on the doorstep. She took one step inside and stopped, gaping at whatever she saw. He shifted uncomfortably. "No one has entered since she died. There will be dirt and dust."

"I'm sure it will be fine. It's just so big! When you said midden, I was picturing something...smaller. I thought of a stasher's nest, if I'm being honest," she said, naming one of the ubiquitous, busy rodents that haunted the city's alleyways and the forests' undergrowth.

"It's small for a Skarr," he chuckled. "But if you will tell me what you need to be comfortable, I will bring it to you."

"I'll make do. It's only temporary, right? I can endure anything for one night. I've slept in far worse." Maja smiled at him over her shoulder.

He sank to his knees right there, humbled by her willingness to suffer for him, even in small ways. "I will not cheat you of this, sweet one. Let me care for you. Treasure you as you should be treasured, gift you and guard you. I didn't begin as I should have, but now I will show you what it is to be a Skarr mate. And if you insist you are human and don't need these things, then do it for me. I need to know you are comfortable and safe."

"Okay," she agreed breathlessly, her cheeks growing pink. She slipped into the midden's dim interior, and Patrek waited patiently there on his knees, listening to her tiny sounds of interest and surprise, a suppressed sneeze, a grunt and scrape as she moved things around. The sounds of his mate nesting made his smile grow.

She emerged a short while later with spinnerwebs in her head fur and a smudge on her cheek, her eyes bright. "It's amazing," she breathed. "I can't believe what's in here. All her work. There's a seed bank, Patrek. There are maps of breeding grounds and population counts for so many species. Records of the weather, changes in the paths of rivers and streams, when the flowers bloomed and when the fruit ripened and when the leaves fell. How did Brannica *do* all this?"

"She was the last of her kind," he explained sadly. "When the Skarr thrived, all the females worked together, pooling their observations from their territories. You're seeing the work of many generations."

"Who's doing it now?" she demanded. He just shook his head. "*Someone* must be doing it!"

"We're trying," he said simply. "Skarr senses what they are, we males do not have the same sensitivity as our females had, so we employ other ways. You've seen our efforts. We work with the Authority and the Council to limit human and Nightborn expansion. We lobby to limit the conversion of forest to farmland. We expose dealers in rarer species. Rehabilitate creatures we've rescued from the black markets. We only have one generation left to set up protections for Salaan before the Skarr are gone forever."

"We can do more. We *have* to do more," she insisted.

If she didn't fit in his palm, he'd say her heart was bigger than any Skarr he knew. "I agree with you, sweet one. We will, I promise you. But tonight is about you and your comfort."

"*Our* comfort," she corrected immediately. He could tell she would not bend on this, so he just nodded and waited to hear her needs, though his own comfort was the last thing on his mind. "I could use a step or ladder of some kind to reach the high places," she ventured shyly. "And the bed is quite dusty, so fresh blankets would be nice, although—"

"You will have them," he interrupted. "Anything else?"

Her cheeks colored slightly. "Water, for bathing? And something to eat, if you don't mind. And a light of some kind?"

"It is my duty and honor to bring you these things," he said, the odd formality a tight skin that barely contained his burgeoning pleasure at being at her service. He had never felt such satisfaction. Not at a fight won, not at saving a vulnerable creature, not even at spilling all over Maja's sweet form in the silvery moons-light. This was beyond all that. It was now his reason for being.

Alrek was right—he had cheated them both out of this.

He left to gather what she needed. What she *required*. And being her requirement made him delirious. So delirious that when Arngar, a kithood friend, stopped him and asked what humans liked to eat, he answered truthfully. "A bit of everything, it seems."

"But her *favorite*?" Arngar pressed, his sandy-brown face plates grinding impatiently. "Does she like sweet things? She didn't say."

Patrek blinked away his daydreams, surprised. "You were listening?"

"We couldn't help but hear. You've spent too long among dull-sensed creatures." Arngar gestured, and Patrek realized that at least four other Skarr were standing around like boulders, waiting for his answer to Arngar's question, and a few others were carrying stacks of soft skins out of their dens, headed toward the midden where he'd just left Maja.

They were *gifting her*.

"No!" he growled, every fiber of muscle in his body pulled tight at once, as though the five spires of stone around them had curled into a jealous fist that he now wielded. "Maja is *mine*. I hunted her. I found her by her scent and now she wears my oils. And if any one of you touches even a tuft of her head fur, you will find out how hot my instincts burn for her. I will *destroy* you, Skarr loyalty be damned."

"The human asked to bathe," Arngar argued, practically begging to have his skull smashed, speaking of her that way. "We all heard it. If she washes away your oils, my instincts may flare for her, too. It can happen with willing females that more than one male burns for them." One of his cousins nearby barked agreement, and Patrek's fists squeezed with the effort of keeping them at his sides.

A heavy hand came down on his shoulder before he could do anything as stupid as start a fight while Maja was alone, waiting for him in the dusty dark. It was his brother, the Corek-cursed, bitter bastard.

"Did you goad them into this to sabotage me?" Patrek roared, fury running in his veins, replacing the blood that should have bound the two brothers together.

"No. I wouldn't try to steal your happiness. I know what it is to find a true mate." Alrek gave him a sideways, serious look even as he squeezed Patrek's shoulder with a gentleness that felt shockingly like sympathy. "As your brother, I am glad you found her. But with her, you brought hope to your brethren of finding the same. I speak as your clan chief when I say that you must allow them this opportunity to court her. Until you have completed the ritual, they have every right to offer her what she needs, just as she has every right to choose someone other than you, if they please her more. It is our way. Remember, Brannica had at least a dozen suitors when she picked me."

Patrek growled and shrugged him off, hating that what he said was true. "Maja already chose me in her human way."

"If it is as you say, you have nothing to fear. Of course, you cannot tell her which gifts are yours, so I suggest you please her as I did my mate. By gifting well, not by rumbling around like an avalanche." Was that humor twinkling in Alrek's eye? Patrek had not seen a spark like that since before Brannica fell ill. It was almost worth this torture of watching other males gift his mate, seeing his brother happy, even if the joke was at his own expense.

"How?" Patrek begged. "How did you make sure she chose you when she did not know which gifts were yours? These saltlickers heard everything Maja asked for!"

"It was elannot pollen," Alrek said, a sad smile playing on his lips. "Brannica loved it. She always carried some with her, and it calmed her to smell it.

I dusted it over everything, so she couldn't help but choose my pile because it already smelled like *hers*. If you love this human, you know what she loves most, even if she did not say it. Give her what she wants, not just what she asked for. Hurry, now. You are the only one without a pile started."

Patrek obeyed, buoyed by Alrek's encouragement. But his heart sank as he went to his den and saw the state of his own furs. Dusty as the trail they'd taken up to the Hand, and he did not have time to clean them. Little better than the ones in the midden, he guessed. He would not let Maja choose someone else, though. It would devastate her as much as it would him.

But just as he was preparing to storm across the meadow and carry her off, Alrek appeared in the doorway, his arms full of clean, plush skins, undoubtedly from his own bed.

"I would gift her these if my tusk did not pain me still," he said, holding them out. "Your human will make a fine Skarr mate."

From any other male, it would have sparked Patrek's possessive instinct, but from his brother and clan chief, it was the highest compliment. He pulled

Alrek into a rough embrace, the bedding caught between them. "Thank you. I did not expect this from you. I was ready to break with the clan or break a tusk myself if she left me, nothing in between."

"My heart is not made of stone. Not entirely, anyway. I can't give you any more advantages, though," Alrek said gruffly, pushing the skins on him as he turned to leave. "I'm sorry I can't stay to see whether she chooses you or not. I need—" His voice thickened and cut off, and he left without finishing his thoughts. Patrek knew where he was going, though. To visit his mate and sit by her cairn, guarding even during her longest rest.

Patrek's focus narrowed to the female whose tiny form was already carved on his soul. He rolled up the softest of Alrek's skins, thinking of how they would cushion and warm her as she slept, and stacked them alongside the growing piles of other males' gifts.

They were already getting it wrong, he noticed, leaving naka nuts in their knobby shells that were too strong for human teeth to crack. Carra roots in their leathery peels too thick for human claws to pierce. Bundles of crisp sansibar leaves, which, though delicious when cooked and a favorite of their females, were furred with fine hairs sure to sting Maja's sensitive hide.

They were bringing gifts for any female, not *this* female. Not *his* female.

Patrek skinned a single carra root and put it to roast in Alrek's hearth while he scoured the forest. He chose the sweetest brindleberries, the ones too small to be of notice to most Skarr, fumbling them in his thick fingers until he'd collected a palmful. He found a hollow log full of onga syrup and took some of that for her, too, swatting away the insects' buzzing protests. He combined the cooked carra with the bright berries and glistening, golden syrup in a small bowl. Small for a Skarr, anyway, but as big as Maja's head. It might look pitiful compared to the mountains of food that Arngar was assembling, but he knew she'd enjoy every bite.

He fulfilled her requests, too, locating a lightweight footstool that could be her ladder and a basin of clean water for her bath, arranging them all in a way he hoped would please her, lit by lanterns with fresh candles burning in them. And while the other males decorated their towering piles with pollen and petals, Patrek knew that Maja's heart would beat faster for something very different. Something only he could provide.

Chapter 15

MAJA

Light was fading and dusk settling in when a heavy knock came at the door of the midden, jolting Maja from her absorption in Brannica's journal. The enormous pages took both hands and all her strength to turn, but she had been instantly drawn in by the Skarr female's careful observations of the forest's species, her simple, evocative sketches of their life cycles, and her ideas for how to protect and increase populations that had been endangered by agricultural expansion into their habitats.

She slid down from where she'd been perched to read, eager to rinse away some of the day's grime and eat whatever she'd smelled cooking through the open window. She smiled as she opened the door, expecting to see Patrek kneeling before it. But he was standing quite far away, far enough that she had to squint to make him out in the dusk.

Between them lay at least a half-dozen huge heaps, each taller than she stood and illuminated by circles of candles that came up to her knees, flickering in dishes and lanterns. Not just one step ladder as she'd requested, but all kinds—stones and log rounds and more refined furniture sized for someone much larger. Not a single meal, but more fruits and vegetables than she could eat in three lifetimes. Not a few blankets, but stacks of them, enough to fill the midden to the ceiling. Vats of water she could practically swim in.

She laughed at the excess. "You did all this for me?" she called to her sweet, generous giant.

"*We* did." He gestured, and she realized that the stones wreathed in fog that stood around him were in fact the other Skarr males, the ones who'd hidden away out of respect for her earlier. "They wished to gift you, too. To court you. And now you must choose which gifts to accept, sweet Maja. Who will have the honor of guarding you tonight?"

They *all* courted her? She had not expected this part of the ritual to be a test, and her anxiety grew, her heart speeding as she considered what might happen if she chose incorrectly. There were many levels of consent in their ritual, she remembered from Patrek's description. She would be in no danger if she picked another giant and could simply decline. But she did not want to give the clan an excuse to doubt their connection by choosing someone else's gift.

"Which pile is yours?" she asked, circling the one nearest. It glittered with pollen so thick that it tickled her nose.

"You must choose the gifts that please you most," came his dissatisfied rumble, and she could tell he was holding back a calming coo, having sensed her dismay. The other males made noises of tense agreement, and it seemed the whole meadow held its breath, waiting for her to choose.

For a brief while, she delayed her decision. She took her time examining each pile of gifts in turn, smelling the flowers that adorned them, petting the soft furs, and complimenting the arrangement and contents, still worried that she might pick wrong. That she might confuse someone else's gifts for his, because they all seemed the same. But then she saw it. Atop the smallest pile lay a single white feather that could only have come from a gharial. He must have saved it, tucked away in a pocket or pack, to remember her sweet friend, Carra. And she knew that she never could have blundered. Patrek would always be unmistakably hers.

"I choose the male who left these," she said proudly, and the meadow let out its collective breath. "I am honored by all of your gifts, though. You have done so well, and I thank each of you for your care. Any female would be proud to call you her mate."

"But only one calls you his." Patrek scooped her up before she knew it, settling her in his lap and swathing her in furs to eat a delicious, sticky, berry-studded concoction he'd prepared. When she was fed and warm, the other Skarr approached one at a time to meet her, kneeling a distance away and speaking in soft tones as they introduced themselves, shyly calling her sister and friend before excusing themselves to dismantle to gift piles they'd assembled.

"Why don't they come near?" she asked Patrek at one point, when two Skarr skirted them widely as they hauled items back to their dens.

"They don't want to scare you off now that you've nested here," he said, stroking her head and down her back, sending a rush of sensation through her. Then he added with a chuckle, "Nor will they risk coming within range of my fists. I'm feeling quite possessive of you, little heart."

"Well, you have me now. I'm all yours." She sighed happily and felt his impossibly huge cock, which she'd been using as a back rest, pulse in reply. She turned her head and gave it an impulsive kiss through his trousers, and he groaned.

"Now I must guard you all night while he howls at me because he can't have you."

"Can't he?" she asked, pressing her back against him. She could feel his olje gush, the warm oils spreading through the fabric, and answering moisture bloomed between her thighs. "I think he has a very good chance if he asks nicely."

"We are doing things the right way this time. You must rest first," he said firmly, putting his hand between them to stop her teasing. "Each step serves an important purpose. I hope you sleep well tonight, Maja, because this phase of the ritual will prepare you for the next, which is much less restful."

She bit her lip against the tide of heat that surged over her, remembering his whispered words in her basement apartment, promises of pinning and rutting. Though they sounded impossible at the time, out of reach for someone like her, with Patrek, anything was possible.

Warmed in every way, she let him guard her while she bathed under the open sky, now studded with more stars than she'd ever seen from a city window. Let him hold the lantern to light her path while she moved her new blankets and animal skins into the midden. Held onto his tusks and kissed him over and over until he pushed her inside, laughing, and closed the door so she'd go to bed. And when she laid in the huge, soft nest, it felt like a dream even before she shut her eyes.

Maja woke to birdsong, and for a minute she thought the sound was her heart begging to fly out of her chest in anticipation of what the day would bring. Was it only yesterday they had escaped the city in the dim hours of early morning? She never realized how caged she'd been until she was truly free.

Outside, she heard Patrek shift his heavy limbs, his coo unspooling in the fresh morning air. It melted her into the bed, pushing her down into drowsy pleasure until it felt like she was floating on the furs. He must have sensed her waking, heard her pulse quicken when she remembered where she was and how her life had changed overnight, and wanted to calm her.

His face appeared at the window, breath moving the stiff, woven curtains as he rested his tusks on the sill. "I will take care with you, Maja," he said. "You don't have to worry."

"I know you will," she said, pushing up so she could see him better, still slightly breathless from how the sound had dismantled her. "I'm excited, not scared. Where are we doing this? In here? Or are we going somewhere else? Don't tell me it's outside in front of everyone..."

His head fell back momentarily as he boomed a laugh. "Eager heart. First, I must feed you again. And then you will choose the place. I will make you a nest of furs or flowers or moss. I'll carry you to a mountaintop or down to the sea. Wherever and whatever you wish."

"I just want you to take me home," she said, climbing over the end of the bed to the windowsill so she could lean out on his tusks and kiss him. "To *our* home, where we'll stay together."

"My den is nothing much," he said, doubt lacing through his tone.

"It's everything to me," she said. "I've never had one."

"Not many Skarr dens in the city." His face was so close to hers she could barely focus on his wry smile.

"A home, Patrek. I've had places to sleep sometimes, like my last apartment, but I've never had anywhere I felt secure. Where I wouldn't be turned out in days or weeks if I didn't grasp and scramble for every credit. Where I wasn't at the whim of someone heartless or careless or both."

His low, possessive growl made her quake with desire for him, and his growl shifted to something else when he caught the scent of her arousal. "*Mate*," he breathed, leaning toward her through the window frame, his thick tongue slipping out to stroke down her neck, dipping beneath the neckline of her sleeping shift. Her nipples tightened, and the sharp sensation reminded her that they had a ritual to fulfill.

"Go get my breakfast," she ordered, pushing his tusks back out the window. "I don't want to wait any longer." She enjoyed the sound of his laughter as he crossed the meadow. She dressed and waited for him outside the midden. He returned with a bowl of warm, cooked grains that could have fed her whole apartment building. She sat in his lap near the riverbank, doing her best to eat with the spoon as large as her arm.

"I might need to get some human-sized things," she said, when she'd eaten as much as she could.

"Today?" he asked, sounding alarmed.

She giggled at him and put aside what was left of the food, her belly pleasantly tight. "No. Today I think I'd like everything to be Skarr-sized."

Beside her, his cock jumped, knocking her elbow. "He thinks you're talking about him," Patrek chuckled.

Maja turned to face him, gripping the base of it between her knees as she gazed up at his amused expression. "I was. I am. Take me home, Patrek."

This time he didn't delay, didn't try and spoil her further, didn't argue her choice of location or press her to choose something more elaborate or luxurious. He simply carried her across the meadow to a cave in the Thumb. It was beautiful inside, full of sturdy wooden furniture and shelves of books, with smooth stone walls and a high, arched ceiling hung with lanterns. Smaller, rougher passageways branched off from the main cavern, but Patrek took her straight to the boat-sized bed in an alcove at the back that was as large as her whole apartment in the city.

"Alrek must have freshened the furs for us," he said, sounding surprised as he laid her out in them. "He's not all growl, I promise. Once you come to know him, he isn't so bad."

"I like your brother," Maja reassured him, thinking of what she'd read in Brannica's journal about the depth of Alrek's care for his mate. How he'd showered her with gifts and protected her from any harm, no matter how slight. Stood by her even when she couldn't give him a kit, even when she was so ill that he had to tend her every need. Any male who treated his female so well was good at his core, even if he flung boulders and accusations when he thought his people were being threatened. "Alrek listened to me when he believed I was an enemy. He put aside his own feelings to give me a chance."

"He's a good chief and a good brother," Patrek agreed gruffly, smoothing the soft bedding around her, tracing the outline of her body with one thick finger. "But I don't want to talk about him."

She squirmed as he brushed along her sensitive ribs. "What do you want to talk about?"

"This," he said, and a blink later he'd dropped over her, a tusk on either side of her waist, pinning her into the furs. "Us," he added, breath hot on her belly.

Chapter 16

PATREKILGAR

He could not get enough of her. Never enough. Even this close, knowing Maja was all his, he was dizzy with need for more. She trembled, blooming, turning pink around the edges under his avid gaze.

"What's next?" she asked in a whisper, gripping his tusks like she was keeping him there instead of being kept.

He'd gifted and guarded her. Calmed her and fed her. Took her home when she asked, when she *offered* herself, as though the ritual came as naturally to her as it did to him.

"Oils," he said hoarsely. The only thing that could make her scent more perfect was combining it with his. She nodded, wriggling out of her sleeping shift in one movement using some kind of intoxicating female magic. Her tiny, soft body on full display, he ran his tongue between her breasts, the tip of it pushing them apart. "You want them here?"

She nodded, biting her lip as her heart sped until it was musical in his ears like a busy onga hive, and he swept his tongue lower over the swell of her belly.

"Here?"

"Yes."

Lower still, tucking between her thighs so he could taste her salty, slippery folds as she spread her legs to give him better access. She arched up, levering her hips against his soft, sensitive muscle, groaning at the rough texture as she dragged herself over it again and again.

"*Yes, yes, yes.*"

He reached to unfasten his belt, dipping inside his trousers to roughly collect oils from his eager olje. He pressed her to the bed with his tongue, stilling her even as she panted and arched and gripped his tusks. Then, he stroked the oils over her body, gently massaging his scent into her skin. A task that would take two hands if he had a Skarr female pinned by the neck took only one reverent finger.

Her taste still on his tongue, he traced the delicate lines of her face, her smooth, perfect forehead. Her lips, both impossibly tiny and impossibly full. The gentle curve of her cheek. She leaned into him, her eyes closing in bliss as his oils began to soothe and calm her. Her neck, slim as a sansibar stem, and her shoulders. He thumbed the oils across her breasts, leaving them glistening like opals, and then did the same to her arms, covering them in one motion from shoulder to wrist. Then he drew a silky line down her belly, pulling a breathy sigh out of her.

He teased her legs farther apart, coating her folds, drinking up every little noise she uttered as he made sure every part of her carried his scent, even using his littlest finger to put some inside her. She made a noise of complaint when he pulled it out again, but he had to finish the task. He was *compelled* by some ancient desire so fundamental to his being that it could not be denied.

As he covered her rounded thighs, her adorable knees, her firm calves, her miniscule toes, he could not help speaking aloud the words that were crowding his thoughts. "You're mine. *Mine.* From now until Salaan swallows me, I will treasure you and protect you, calm you and care for you. Anything you need, you will have from my hands, do you understand? You will drink from my cup and eat from my plate and ride on my shoulders and wear my scent. No one else. And I am yours completely. My tusks are at your service, my body is at your command, and I burn only for you. I love you, little heart."

"Oh, Patrek," she murmured, voice liquid honey. "I love you so much. You'll spoil me, if you're not careful."

The thought of her, so ripe and perfect beneath him, as something rotten made him laugh. "Never. Whatever I can give you, it will never be enough. You are so rare, little heart, that you deserve the moons. If I could pluck Manna and Corek out of the sky for you to wear as earrings, I would."

She slid her hands up his tusks to cradle his jaw, and he rejoiced as a fresh breath of their mingled scent met his lungs now that even the soles of her feet smelled of him. "If you said you could, I would believe it. Now stop teasing me and rut me as you promised," she ordered like a clan chief.

Patrek's unruly cock twitched beneath him, begging to sink into her. It was an impossibility, but so was finding a mate, and here he had one, ordering him to rut her. He'd promise to oblige her in every way, so he kicked out of his trousers and moved up the bed, bracing himself on his elbows to hold his body above her even as he slid his greedy cock alongside her in the furs.

A pair of gorgeous arms tightened around it, just under the head, and he felt his olje spark and flood fresh oils, glossing her breasts as Maja pressed against him. She threw one leg over his shaft so her limb was trapped against his belly, mimicking how she'd gripped and ridden him when he'd belted her into his trousers.

Though he couldn't see her, he could feel every swell and dip of her body as he began to move, rubbing against her, careful not to crush her even as the fog of his rut thickened. He was so in tune with her that he swore he could even feel the beads of her nipples harden and her breaths grow shallow and fast as she angled her hips against him so every stroke pleased her, too.

"Feels so good," she moaned. "You're rutting every part of me, all at once."

Corek, he wasn't going to last. Even though his ears popped with the effort it took to hold back, he knew he had to, at least as long as it took her to find her release. "Tell me what you need, love."

"Faster, harder," she begged, tightening her grip on him. "Don't be so gentle with me."

He bore down slightly, knowing she was cushioned by the thick furs and blankets beneath her, and quickened his hips. It felt so good to him, too, that he still had to use all his strength to stay himself from spilling. His jaw ached from grinding his teeth with the effort. She was so warm and wriggly and slick, so perfect beyond imagination as he rutted her, that at her first jerky *yes*, he was done for.

Pleasure seared up his spine, tightening his balls to boulders as he erupted like a damned volcano, hot and loud. Maja shuddered on and on with her own climax, and he couldn't stop his thrusts from growing more powerful, driving his seed into the furs above her head.

When he was so empty it felt like he was turned inside out, he rolled over, pulling her on top of him to rescue her from the lake he'd produced. She curled up happily on his chest, her fingers tucking between the plates over his heart, like they were the key to unlock it.

"Manna save me if it's like that every time," she said. His momentary jolt of concern was soothed by her scent, which was nothing but sweetness braided with his oils, so he held back his ready coo. He stroked her back, waiting for her to explain. "I've never been so happy in my life. I think I could die of it. What did I do to deserve all this? What did I do to deserve *you*?"

His instincts flared so bright inside his chest that it seared his senses. He knew she'd had a hard life, one where scarcity and cruelty were daily expectations, but he somehow hadn't realized until that moment how it had shaped her self-image. The thought that Maja might believe herself unworthy of a caring mate—something *every* female deserved? It made him gloriously, jubilantly *furious*. He felt downright *vengeful*. His hands ached to crush anyone who had damaged her spirit this way.

But his hands could be put to better use when they held something so precious. When he could catch his breath again, he said, "I will show you every day what you deserve, little heart. Never doubt that you're worthy of every comfort and pleasure on Salaan, and I plan to gift you every day like it's our mating day."

"I'll walk out every afternoon to a pile of fruit outside my door?" she asked, giggling.

"Fruit and furs and gharial feathers, hot water for your bath, human things to fit your tiny hands. Whatever you need. I'll protect you every night like it's our mating night, and pleasure you every morning until you're hoarse from calling my name." Big promises, but he was a Skarr. Everything about him was big, including his promises.

"Won't you be too tired to rut me if you never sleep?" she teased.

He growled at her just to hear her laugh. "I don't need to sleep at night. Not when every day is the best dream I've ever had."

"Mine, too. I was thinking the same thing last night."

He lifted her from his chest to seat her on his chin instead, looping her legs over his tusks so she straddled his face, her heels brushing his earlobes. He couldn't resist a taste, his tongue slipping out to lick up her inner thigh. Salty, sweet, her, him. A *gift*. A *feast*, and his hungry tongue was suddenly as unmanageable as his cock, pushing its way between her legs, seeking and savoring every bit of her he could.

Maja leaned back slightly, bracing herself against his tusks, and it felt like they must have grown there for that purpose and no other. He licked her, ravenous, until she writhed and shuddered and kicked his ears and her arms gave out. He held her in place so she wouldn't fall, pleasing her until she begged him to stop.

Then he cradled her in his hands, covered her with the softest fur on the bed, smiled to himself as her eyelids drooped and her face smoothed with the first gentle brush of sleep. He would guard her until she woke. And though his tongue cried for another taste and his cock fiercely craved another touch, he had never felt more satisfied.

Epilogue

MAJA

Weeks Later

The seasons had begun to shift in the mountains, and the daylight slipped away more quickly than Maja had anticipated. By the time she coaxed the injured stasher out of the hollow log, the golden song of late afternoon had faded to the purple whispers of dusk.

A quick examination proved that the poor thing's leg was only sprained, not broken, but he looked painfully thin, the injury clearly preventing his normal foraging activity. She couldn't leave him to heal on his own. The small rodent's high metabolism meant that he should consume his body weight in grain each day, so nutrition was of utmost importance to his recovery.

With the small creature tucked into her satchel, she hurried back toward Skarr's Hand. It still felt unnatural to be out after dark, but she no longer looked over her shoulder or ducked at every shadow. There were no Nightborn roosts this high in the mountains, and even if there were, she knew the giants of Skarr's hand would protect her with their lives.

Her sense of safety increased the closer she got to home, so much so that she took a tiny detour on the way, crossing the meadow to collect moss from the riverbank and visit a patch where tall graingrass grew. She gathered a handful of the ripe seed heads for the stasher to eat. With a full belly and its leg properly treated with a poultice and a moss-cushioned splint, it might be feeling well enough to release into the sanctuary tomorrow.

The Skarr sanctuary was not what Maja had pictured when Patrek had spoken of it in the city. There were no orderly enclosures or sterile cages. It was simply the meadows and forests surrounding the Hand, where the Skarr could look after animals that needed extra feeding and care to survive. Creatures who required more help found their way into the dens and often the laps of the gentle giants, whose protective instincts, Maja had learned, extended to everything, even the tiny boring beetles that pillaged their wooden furniture.

When she reached the Thumb, she paused in the twilit entrance of their den to fully enjoy the feeling of coming home. The welcoming scent of carra-root stew bubbling on the stove was a perfect complement to the crisp autumn evening. It meant the care of her giant, who'd undoubtedly made it to her tastes. Patrek, it turned out, was an excellent cook, and had made it is his mission to introduce her to every food she'd missed out on in all her twenty-eight summers of life. The stew meant a full stomach and cozy safety.

But it was no match for the warmth of her mate's voice as he hummed a tune, singing snatches of the song as he puttered around the den, readying it for her. He had many missions lately, all of which seemed to revolve around her happiness. As if she could get any happier!

"I can hear your pretty pulse quickening," he called from inside, a smile in his voice. "What thrills you, little heart? Will I be tasting dinner next or will it be something else on my tongue?"

She laughed, stepping through the doorway and into the glowing circle of light thrown by the many onga-wax candles he'd lit on their dinner table. It was far too large for her to sit at, but she preferred to eat in his lap, anyway, as she had on their mating day. "I think one and then the other. I have to ensure my mountain doesn't waste away if I'm going to keep him up all night."

"If I must," he grumbled good-naturedly as he ladled out bowls of stew, a human-sized one for her and a vat for himself, and set them on the table. "Who is our guest tonight?"

Of course, he'd found her out by sound or smell or some other Skarr sense. She brought out the little stasher, who huddled in her palm, his mustache-like brush of whiskers trembling. "He only has a sprain, but look at his ribs! He hasn't been eating well."

Patrek nodded. "Then he must stay until he's fat and fit. Do I need to finish another side passage?" Patrek had taken it upon himself to add several more rooms to the spacious den since she moved in, enough that she could bring home as many creatures as needed a place to rest and recover safely. They were all full at the moment, though, and she worried her lip, thinking of where to put the small stasher. She poured the handful of grassgrain she'd collected onto the tabletop and placed him gently down beside it. He instantly picked up one of the fat seedheads and stuffed it into his cheek. A second went in the other cheek pouch. Then he snatched a third and began to nibble at it voraciously.

"I think he'll be fine in a less permanent accommodation. A basket by the fire, maybe?"

Patrek was already reaching up to take down a basket from one of the ceiling hooks. A minute later, he'd lined it with one of his handknit scarves and added a small bowl of water beside it and a crust of a freshly baked loaf tucked into the soft interior. Not proper nutrition for a stasher, but an indulgence she wouldn't deny either of them. She knew by now that her giant *needed* to do this, needed to protect and provide, as much as the injured rodent needed to be protected and provided for. Maybe more. "That's perfect."

"I think I should finish another passage or two anyway. You bring home a new houseguest nearly every day. They'll be taking over our bed before we know it," he mused to himself, sounding proud rather than annoyed. Maja bit her lip against her smile and let him putter about with his plans while she got the stasher settled in his new, temporary nest.

When the little creature was fed and stowed away in a warm nook, its cheeks fat with the leftover grain, Maja enjoyed her stew and bread in her Patrek's broad, comfortable lap, bracketed by his strong arms as he ate his own meal.

"Don't drip or I might drown in your dinner," she warned him when his shovel-sized spoon swooped over her head.

"I'd clean you up like I always do," came his smug reply, and when she looked at him, he gave his spoon a wicked lick to illustrate. She felt heat bloom all over her body that wasn't from the roaring hearth.

"You're so good to me," she said, leaning into him when she'd finished eating. He was her home. Her mountain.

He lifted her to his chest and held her there over his huge, honorable heart. She wedged her fingers between his rocky plates so she could feel it beating through his skin. The rush and thump of it spelled the truth. He was hers and she was his, forever.

Thank you for journeying to the mountains with Maja and Patrek! I hope you fell in love with them and their sweet, fluffy, mismatched romance as much as I did. If you're inclined, a review is greatly appreciated!

If you'd like to see an illustration I doodled of the apartment scene, with Maja perched "like a blossom" on Patrek's branch, you can download it (and a printable coloring sheet version) when you subscribe to my newsletter: https://bookhip.com/PLTLFJK

Want to read more?

The salt planet of Salaan occupies a huge portion of my imagination, and I'm excited to set more stories in this world. If you'd like to visit it again, you can!

THE BALLAST'S BRIDE (Salt Planet Giants Book 2)

He'll cross oceans for his mate...

Skarr giant Hinrivik has been in love with the human he guards for years. But when her marriage is arranged—and he's assigned to deliver her to her groom across the sea—he loses hope that she'll ever return his feelings.

When they cross the ocean, she'll step off the ship into her new life as someone else's wife. Can Hinrivik convince her to consider him, a wildly mismatched monster, as her mate? He'll have to do it before they reach the other shore...because breaking her marriage contract could easily start a war.

The Ballast's Bride is a sweet and steamy size-difference alien romance about a gentle giant bodyguard and the tiny human woman who ignites his instincts.

Find it here: https://www.amazon.com/dp/B0B JC816N3

BOUND BY THE ALIEN KING

On the other side of the Salten Sea, humans and Nightborn don't mingle—not until an ancient treaty requires the alien king to take a human wife. Too bad he's fallen for another female...a broken one who washed up in his territory and threatens to destroy the tenuous peace between their species.

You can read it for free if you subscribe to my newsletter: https://bookhip.com/DFVNNPF

Or find it on Amazon, where it's also available in paperback: https://www.amazon.com/dp/B0BJ 23HW1H

Other Books

The Warrior Kings of Alioth Series

The Emperor of the Five Planets is dead. One of his sons will rise to rule. Abducted women meet their fated mates in this steamy, sci-fi romance series set in a solar system of barbarian planets ruled by arrogant alien kings!

Stolen by Starlight (Book 1) — Lothan and Ada

Stained by Starlight (Book 2) — Thren and Bree

Scorched by Starlight (Book 3) — Kyaal and Jaya

Seduced by Starlight (Book 4) — Coming in 2023

Sparked by Starlight (Book 5) — Coming in 2023

Saved by Starlight (Book 6) — Coming in 2023

Read them all on Amazon (they're free to borrow in Kindle Unlimited)! https://www.amazon.com/dp/B09GRKDZSK

About the Author

USA Today bestselling author Sara Ivy Hill is truly hopeless about staying up past midnight to read by moons-light. She's fascinated by the possibilities of the universe and is certain it's bigger and more magical than anyone on our little planet can imagine. She writes steamy alien romance because love is out there. You can discover her books and connect with her here:

https://linktr.ee/saraivyhill

Made in United States
Troutdale, OR
11/04/2024